DOCTOR WHO NOVELLAS

FOREIGN DEVILS

Andrew Cartmel

TELOS
.CO.UK

First published in England in 2003 by
Telos Publishing Ltd
61 Elgar Avenue, Tolworth, Surrey KT5 9JP, England
www.telos.co.uk

ISBN: 1-903889-33-2 (paperback)
Foreign Devils © 2002 Andrew Cartmel
Dragon motif © 2002 Nathan Skreslet

The moral rights of the author have been asserted

'DOCTOR WHO' word mark, device mark and logo are trade marks of the British Broadcasting Corporation and are used under licence from BBC Worldwide Limited. Doctor Who logo © BBC 1996. Certain character names and characters within this book appeared in the BBC television series 'DOCTOR WHO'. Licensed by BBC Worldwide Limited

Font design by Comicraft. Copyright © 1998 Active Images/Comicraft
430 Colorado Avenue # 302, Santa Monica, Ca 90401
Fax (001) 310 451 9761/Tel (001) 310 458 9094
w: www.comicbookfonts.com   e: orders@comicbookfonts.com

Typeset by
TTA Press, 5 Martins Lane, Witcham, Ely, Cambs CB6 2LB, England
w: www.ttapress.com   e: ttapress@aol.com

Printed in India

1 2 3 4 5 6 7 8 9 10 11 12 13 14 15

British Library Cataloguing in Publication Data. A catalogue record for this book is available from the British Library. This book is sold subject to the condition that it shall not by way of trade or otherwise, be lent, resold, hired out or otherwise circulated without the publisher's prior written consent in any form of binding or cover other than that in which it is published and without a similar condition including this condition being imposed on the subsequent purchaser.

DOCTOR WHO™
NOVELLAS

FOREIGN DEVILS

FOREIGN DEVILS

Andrew Cartmel

Prologue

The streets outside the British Concession were full of the smell of firecrackers, fragrant grey smoke swirling over the greasy faces and trembling banners of the excitable mass of rioters. The throng seemed quite prepared to tear any white man to pieces. But Roderick Upcott had applied generous donations of silver in the right places and he knew of a certain concealed exit, several streets away from the front gates of the Concession.

He emerged into shadows and the sound of dripping water and the thick sour odour of drains in the safety of the merchant's district, a few hundred yards from the spot where the nucleus of the riot was still busily churning. They had arrived at dawn, with a hail of cobblestones aimed at the Concession windows, and hadn't let up for a moment since. Upcott set off in the opposite direction from the Concession and soon he had left behind the smell of gunpowder and the sound of angry chanting voices.

As he hurried along, keeping to shadows, he felt in the pockets of his coat for the reassuring shape of his guns, a handsome pair of greatcoat pistols by Adams of London. He believed these would provide him with a way out of any tricky situation, if required.

Fortunately they were not required; another ten minutes of brisk walking and he had located the narrow winding street, the long high wall of whitewashed stone topped with green tiles, and the door with the brass birds embossed on it. All as described in the letter.

He knocked, but there was no response, so he pushed on the door and it opened into the sound of birdsong. Upcott stepped into the cool shade and damp green fragrance of a small garden. A servant bowed before him. The man's eyes were sunk deep in a sallow face that had no more flesh than a skull's. The man's body was equally emaciated. He wore a dirty loincloth of some kind of brown material and his near naked body was little more than a frail boned skeleton. The man trembled as he moved, his pitiful wasted musculature all too obvious and the gaunt serrations of ribs threatening to cut through his thin pale skin.

This spectre moved slowly and painfully, pushing the heavy brass studded door shut again behind Upcott. Finally he bowed and withdrew, trembling.

Upcott turned away from the man, dismissing his appalling condition. Years in the East had accustomed him to the sight of such suffering. The garden was exquisite, a tiny gem dense with shrubs and ornamental trees with silver birdcages hanging from the branches. Brightly coloured birds jostled inside, competing in song. Beneath these, brilliant goldfish darted in a pond and a jovial Chinaman with a long sparse black beard sat waiting on a chair.

He was a fat man with jowls that sagged below the tapered black ends of his moustache, and small, pale, delicate hands. His lavish blue silk robes figured with flowers marked him as a man of considerable wealth. His eyes twinkled as he sprinkled some kind of coarse pink powder from a small white saucer into the pond.

'Fragments of prawn shell,' explained the Chinaman, smiling. He set the saucer aside and bowed to Upcott. 'Part of the diet of my goldfish.' His English was superb, quite the best Upcott had ever heard. The jumped-up little heathen could have held his own in any debate among learned dons at Cambridge. 'They love to eat it,' he explained. 'It's good for the health of their scales and fins.' Upcott looked at the small glowing fish, so deeply golden coloured that they were almost red. They darted eagerly after the crumbs drifting in the pond. He watched them for a moment then he looked up and met the Chinaman's smiling eyes.

'I'm a blunt man,' said Upcott. 'I came here to do business, not talk about your fish.'

The Chinaman smiled at him patiently. 'Come inside and drink tea with me.' He led Upcott into a long narrow room that smelled pleasantly of roasting pork. Despite the tension and potential danger of the situation, the Englishman felt saliva flow in his mouth and heard his stomach rumble. His host smiled at him and gestured for him to sit. The room contained two low sofas set in front of a large wall hanging, and a big black oblong iron box that occupied the centre of the rug-covered wooden floor. The box was about two feet high by eight feet long and six wide. Silk pillows were strewn across the broad iron lid of the box, turning it into a sort of wide bench. Upcott moved to sit on one of the sofas, but his host gestured instead to the bench. The Chinaman sat down at one end and Upcott perched tentatively at the other.

'Nice and warm, yes?'

'Yes,' said Upcott. The iron box apparently contained some kind of oven and as a consequence the broad bench was pleasantly warm with a strong, subdued and even heat. The warmth gradually crept into his muscles and soon he found himself relaxing onto the cushions. Trust the Chinese to think up such sybaritic comforts to ease a man's existence. He looked at his host sitting opposite him on the big iron box, smiling at him, steadily and silently. The delicious roast pork smell seemed even thicker now. Upcott's mouth watered once more. He wondered if the old boy's hospitality would extend to offering him dinner.

The light in the room was dim and it took a moment for Upcott to register the design on the wall hanging behind the Chinaman. When he did, he felt a sudden cold pulse of disquiet. Woven on the rich cloth was the image of a wildly sprawling green dragon. It was fiercely and finely executed and Upcott knew every curve and coil of its scaled length.

He knew it because he had the same identical image tattooed on his torso, winding up over his chest and onto his back. How strange. The same creature exactly. The coincidence seemed somehow menacing. A cold sweat began flowing down Upcott's ribs, over the colours of that very tattoo. He told himself not to be a fool. It was merely a traditional design. The coincidence meant nothing.

'Tea will be brought to us shortly,' said the Chinaman, breaking the silence. 'I trust you will enjoy my modest offering of hospitality.'

'You can keep your tea,' said Upcott. 'It's not tea I've come here to talk about.'

'No?' His host smiled.

'No, it's not tea that brought me out this afternoon with the streets so unsafe. Tea doesn't yield the sort of profits a businessman in my position demands.'

'Naturally not,' agreed his host.

'My reason for coming here is the same as the reason the streets aren't safe,' said Upcott, smiling at his own wit in noting the parallel.

'Not safe? Really?'

'No. I've got a mob of rioters and troublemakers foaming at the mouth outside the Concession. They've been massing there since dawn and they don't show any signs of going away.'

'And to what do you attribute this minor inconvenience?'

'The activities of the Emperor and his blessed Chief Astrologer, bloody well stirring up trouble again.'

'Ah,' murmured his host. 'The Chief Astrologer. A most interesting man, I believe.'

'Well, he's helping the Emperor kick up a most interesting stink.'

'What a splendid witticism!' exclaimed the Chinaman.

Upcott's brows knotted with suspicion. Was he being mocked? 'What do you mean?'

'Oh, I assumed you knew. It seems the Chief Astrologer has prepared a special mixture to burn, a kind of offertory incense. Which is what I thought you meant by an interesting stink. It is supposed to assist in driving out the Foreign Devil.'

'Which is me, I suppose,' said Upcott. 'What exactly is this mixture?'

'Ginseng, asafoetida, gun powder . . . who knows? I imagine anything that will burn and create smoke with a suitably pungent odour, thus providing the sort of spectacle that will impress and gull the credulous.'

'Gunpowder eh? That must be what I scented on the way here. It's all around the Concession, a billowing great mass of smoke. I thought it was some kind of ground mist.'

'No,' said the Chinaman, shaking his head good naturedly and causing his jowls to wobble. 'Not mist. A smoke created by this charlatan of an Astrologer in his no doubt wholly futile and extravagantly implausible attempt to drive out the European trading interests.'

'Which again is me,' said Upcott. 'Which brings us to the subject of our meeting here today.'

'Opium,' murmured his host smoothly.

'Exactly,' said Upcott. 'The reason for the riots and the reason I'm here. In your letter you said you were interested in buying from me, in bulk and at a premium price.'

'Oh yes,' the man nodded. 'I am sure I will have no difficulty in offering you a better price than any of your other competitors. I have enormous resources at my disposal. You might say they are unlimited.'

The Englishman suppressed a rising, euphoric excitement. If this slippery yellow customer could really offer a higher buying price – say as much as twenty per cent higher than he was getting elsewhere – then it meant Upcott could retire and return to England in no more than two years. Perhaps a year and a half. To be in England again, with a suitable fortune tucked away! And to be shot of this Godforsaken land . . .

The aroma of roast pork in the room had gradually become almost unbearable to a man with Upcott's healthy, not to say ravenous, appetite. But now, as it were, he smelled another aroma which awoke another, even more powerful appetite. He smelled money, and his enormous dormant greed awoke.

He immediately slipped into his most smoothly practised business speech. 'I assure you my company will provide you with only the finest quality Indian opium, rushed by my fleet of clippers from all the choicest sources in the subcontinent. Bombay white skin, Madras red skin, black earth from Patna and Benares. Whatever you desire. All will be yours. My customers,' he purred, 'are always satisfied.'

'I'm sure,' said the Chinaman. 'And speaking of your customers, perhaps you would be good enough to tell me who they are.'

Roderick Upcott was instantly on guard. 'I beg your pardon?'

'Could you kindly give me their names?'

'No. You know I can't do that.'

His host sighed. 'Never mind. I didn't really expect you to.'

'Then why ask?'

The man smiled. 'Perhaps to give you a chance to redeem yourself, however slightly. It was merely a symbolic gesture, of course, since I already have all the names of your customers.'

He reached under the cushions and drew out a shockingly familiar looking book, a large leather-bound ledger the colour of pale toffee with an ornate letter U embossed on its cover. Upcott felt a simultaneous mixture of outrage and alarm.

'Where did you get that?'

His host smiled again and handed him the book. There was an unfamiliar bookmark flapping from the ledger, a broad dark floppy tongue of leather. Upcott seized the book and opened it at the page marked. It was a detailed record of one of his most lucrative transactions to date, describing his meeting with a corrupt mandarin on Lintin Island in the Pearl River estuary, where he had landed and exchanged a hundred chests, a huge amount of smuggled opium, for a proportionately huge quantity of Chinese silver.

Upcott looked up from the ledger. 'Where did you get this?'

'From the premises of your book keeper in Macao, a personage who I am ashamed to acknowledge as one of my countrymen.'

'You broke into his premises?'

'No longer his. His building, business and all his possessions are now forfeit to the Imperial Treasury.' The fat man giggled. 'As is his life.'

'What the blazes do you mean, laughing about it like that?'

The Chinaman gestured at the leathery bookmark that Upcott was holding in his hand. 'It's amusing. Because you are holding his lying tongue in your hand.'

Upcott stared at the bookmark he was holding. It was dried, cured and flattened, but it was still recognisably a human tongue. He muttered an oath and threw it across the room, shuddering with disgust.

The tongue hit the wall hanging of the red dragon and bounced off it, flapping to the floor.

He stared at the Chinaman. 'Who the hell are you?' he demanded.

The Chinaman bowed politely, as though to acknowledge a formal introduction. 'The creator of smoke and stench, the fomenter of riots, the organiser of delightfully unusual meat roasts . . . In short, I am the Chief Astrologer.'

'You!'

'Yes. I must say I greatly enjoyed denigrating myself in the third person.'

'I don't believe you. The Chief Astrologer never leaves the palace.'

'Not never . . . but rarely. I am here on a special mission from the Emperor, who has a particular interest in putting an end to the opium smuggling in his realm.'

'This would be the same smuggling that involves constant bribery that causes silver to pour into the imperial coffers?'

'I'd hardly expect a barbarian like your good self to understand the delicate nuances of such a complex situation.'

Upcott felt a red cloud of rage gathering behind his eyeballs. He felt in his pocket for his pistols. Should he blow this arrogant little monkey to hell? Some tiny voice cautioned him to tread carefully and he gradually he forced himself to relax, releasing the guns again. 'And I suppose none of that silver ever ended up in your purse, fatty? You can't tell me . . .'

Upcott suddenly fell silent.

'Is something wrong?' asked his host solicitously. Upcott didn't reply. He was staring at the wall hanging of the dragon. The one the tongue of his Macao book keeper had just bounced off. The hanging depicted exactly the same dragon which writhed in a tattoo across Upcott's torso, except on a dramatically larger scale, in bright red embroidery.

The problem was, Upcott could have sworn that when he had first entered the room, that dragon had been green.

The damned thing had changed colour. Green to red. Was it some kind of trick? He looked at the Chief Astrologer. His host smiled benignly at him. Some kind of conjuring trick, surely? Some kind of substance that could change colour, embedded in the cloth? He began to sweat. He wouldn't put it past these heathens. They were a tricky lot and loved things like fireworks, which involved cleverness with colours.

Upcott was distracted from these thoughts when a figure appeared silently in the doorway of the room. It was the emaciated wraith of a manservant who had greeted him in the garden. He was carrying an elaborate tea service on an ornate brass tray.

'Don't worry about that now,' said the Chief Astrologer, gesturing the servant away. 'I don't think my guest is in the mood for tea.' He smiled at Upcott as the walking cadaver of the servant lurched across the room to set the tray down on a lacquered sideboard. He was moving with such terrible trembling slowness that it was painful to watch.

'One of the victims of your trade,' said his host in a pleasant, conversational tone of voice.

'What do you mean?'

'He is an addict. A hopeless case. His wife and children starved to death long ago, as a consequence of his habit. He himself will be dead before the moon rises again.' The Chinaman smiled. 'And of course there are many more like him, more than you could count in your lifetime.'

Upcott felt his temper rising again. 'I think you've wasted enough of my time.'

'Why do you say that?'

The Englishman hesitated. 'I was brought here under false pretences.'

'Were you?'

Suddenly Upcott was uncertain. 'Wasn't that letter, the letter inviting me here, just a fraud to draw me out?'

His host shook his head, jowls wobbling. 'Not at all. The offer and the merchant making it were both entirely genuine.' The Chief Astrologer gestured around at the room they were sitting in. 'The owner of this charming house and delightful garden with such marvellous goldfish was indeed eager to meet you and do business.' He smiled. 'Unfortunately the poor fellow is no longer in a position to offer you the generous terms that lured you to this rendezvous.'

'Really? What has become of him?'

'Oh, he is proving useful.' The Chief Astrologer patted the wide iron bench on which they were sitting. 'Don't you find it delightfully warm, sitting on this contraption?'

Upcott felt a liquid shudder of premonition. The roast pork smell was suddenly thick in his nostrils. His mouth had gone dry and sour. Repressing the urge to retch, he stood up, feeling the warmth of the bench clinging to his thighs.

'Yes, the gentleman in question kindly provided the use of his house for our meeting, with all its fine furnishings. Although there was one item of furniture I provided myself.' The Chief Astrologer patted the bench again.

The silent trembling wraith of a servant had finished putting the tea things down and slowly and painfully crossed the room to join them again. His gaze passed over Upcott without fear or hatred or even recognition. The man's eyes were like dead coals in a fire that had long gone out. The Chief Astrologer barked a rapid command at him and the man moved some cushions aside with trembling hands, exposing the outline of a large hinged lid in the surface of the iron bench.

The servant opened the lid and a ferocious burst of heat came wafting out of the oven-like interior. The air over the opening danced, blurring for a moment the hot orange bed of coals that could be glimpsed inside.

And something else, charred and black, with a hint of a paler colour showing through. A colour as pale as ivory, or bone. With a rush of horror Upcott realised it was the blackened, burnt skull of a man. Grinning up at him. A man who had been roasted alive.

He backed away, trying not to gag. 'Good Lord,' he choked. The skull smiled at him from its bed of smouldering coals. 'If you had arrived here an hour earlier,' said his host cheerfully, 'you would have heard him still struggling inside the oven!'

Upcott snatched up the ledger and turned to flee.

'Yes, do take it,' said his host as Upcott turned for the door. 'I have made a copy and the customers who are named in it will soon be suffering most unpleasant fates.'

Upcott lunged through the door.

'Why run off?' called the Chief Astrologer. 'I have no intention of killing you. Your fate will be more far reaching and much worse!' He began to laugh.

His mockery pursued Upcott all the way through the bird-adorned garden, to the brass studded door, and out into the street. Gasping for breath, he gripped his pistols and turned and fled, pursued by the sound of laughter and the ripe sweet stench of roasting meat.

Chapter One

The three of them stood in the control room, peering up at the small screen tucked away high on the wall. They were trying to make out a mist-shrouded image.

Zoe squinted in irritation. 'Don't you have a screen that's a bit bigger?'

'Bigger?' the Doctor seemed puzzled, as if the concept had never occurred to him before. Then, almost as if caused by this puzzlement, a wave of interference passed over the image on the screen, blotting it out altogether.

'Well, it's completely gone now,' said Jamie.

'Yes,' said Zoe. She looked at the Doctor. 'Can't you replace it with something bigger? Bigger and more reliable and with more resolution.'

'Aye. More resolution,' said Jamie. 'That's something any man could do with. I could do with having a bit more resolution myself.'

The Doctor's mercurial attention shifted to the young man. 'Oh I don't know.' He smiled warmly at Jamie. 'I think you've shown considerable resolve when the situation warranted it.'

Zoe was beginning to feel her temper fray. She started casting about for something to throw at the screen. 'I can tell you, we had better equipment than this on the Wheel.'

'You know, come to think of it, I do have a bigger screen,' said the Doctor. 'I took it down for repair one day then somehow forgot to put it back up.'

He pressed a button and suddenly one entire wall of the control room blossomed into a massive glowing screen, displaying an image of pin-sharp clarity. Jamie gawped while Zoe watched with cynical detachment; she was accustomed to sophisticated technology.

The screen revealed a long stone building. It stood two stories high with tall dark recesses of windows and a slanted roof with odd curling tiles. At both ends of the building it was joined by a twin building set perpendicularly to it. The image on the screen roved slowly around, and by the time it settled back to its original point of view, Zoe had a clear idea of the building's structure. It consisted of four long wings joined to form a square. The empty centre of the square was occupied by a large gravelled garden in the centre of which stood the TARDIS.

The walls of the building were slick with rain and gleaming in the early morning sunlight. In the centre of the screen, just outside the TARDIS, stood a flowering cherry tree. Pink petals drifted down onto the gravel.

On the far side of the garden stood a flagpole with a flag flapping on it.

Jamie evidently recognised the flag. 'English,' he said. 'Just my luck.'

'Actually, we're in China, December 1800,' declared the Doctor, reading a string of luminous green hieroglyphics that wormed their way across the top of the screen in a continuous parade. Zoe tried to read the strange symbols but despite her extensive knowledge of languages, she could make nothing of them. The text, if it was text, resembled some kind of primitive cuneiform.

The peaceful image on the screen began to fade away, the courtyard disappearing under a swirl of misty white. 'Picture's going again,' said Jamie.

'Oh Doctor,' said Zoe petulantly.

The Doctor frowned. 'No. There's nothing wrong with it. It's not the screen. What we're seeing is actually out there.' The cherry trees and buildings were now almost completely obscured by the swirling whiteness.

'Mist?' asked Zoe.

'Maybe,' said the Doctor, and punched a button. The door began to buzz open slowly. 'Shall we step out and see?'

Outside the air was cool and heavy with a smell that pinched the throat. 'It's not mist,' said Jamie sniffing. 'It's smoke. Gunpowder.'

Wraiths of smoke floated around them, curling around their legs like a friendly, welcoming cat. The rope rattled against the flagpole with a steady, eerie sound. Zoe looked back at the TARDIS, savouring the Magritte-like incongruity of the English police box in this Chinese garden. 'What do we do now?'

The Doctor was already crunching across the gravel to the cloistered walkway of the low stone building. 'Go in and say hello.'

But before he reached the walkway, a man appeared on it, stepping out of the shadowed interior of the building. 'Who the devil are you lot?' he demanded, brandishing a rifle.

He was a tall man with long auburn hair that continued down the sides of his face in an unbroken flow to transform itself into a long drooping moustache. He was wearing breeches and a white shirt that had recently seen some hard wear; it was virtually slashed to ribbons.

The man's tobacco-brown eyes shone with intelligence and anger. Through the slashes in his shirt Zoe caught glimpses of what looked like a tattoo.

The man raised his rifle to point at them.

'We're visitors,' said the Doctor in a friendly, explanatory fashion. The rifle didn't seem to bother him.

The man squinted at him. The Doctor had a knack for disarming people; sometimes quite literally. Now this man's rifle faltered. He lowered the muzzle until it no longer pointed directly at them.

'Well you'd better come inside,' he said. He glanced uneasily around at the smoke-wreathed garden. The tang of gunpowder still burned the back of Zoe's throat. His gaze settled on her. 'No one's safe with those malevolent yellow fiends on the war path.' He stood aside to let them enter the house, through the tall door that stood open beside him.

Zoe wondered what the man had made of the TARDIS. But as she glanced back she realised it was completely obscured by a billowing cloud of smoke. Then, for the first time, she noticed something else. There was an odd structure at the foot of the garden. Wider than the TARDIS and somewhat taller. She caught a glimpse of what looked like a stone gateway, leading nowhere . . .

Then it was lost from sight and she turned and followed the Doctor and Jamie into the cool dim interior of the building. They entered a long, opulently decorated room. It smelled of dust and sandalwood. Between shuttered windows, the walls were hung with polychromatic rugs and tapestries. The floor was covered with elaborate tasselled carpets but the only actual furniture consisted of a few sofas interspersed with handsome oblong chests made of polished wood. Decorated silk cloths were placed on some of the chests, making them look like elegant tables.

As they entered the room in single file, their host studied them carefully, perhaps struck by the incongruity of their clothing. The Doctor's soup stained jacket and baggy checked trousers were perhaps only anachronistic by a few decades and Jamie's kilt and rough woven sweater might have passed muster in this era, but Zoe was wearing her favourite silver lamé catsuit and it obviously startled the man, revealing as it did the contours of her body in uncensored detail.

Indeed, it seemed he had trouble taking his eyes off her. Finally he looked away and went to the opposite wall, where tall windows were shuttered against the daylight. He opened one shutter a few inches and peered out the small opening. The pearly light of day came through, gleaming on his eyes. 'Quiet out there now,' he declared. 'But I don't trust those little savages for a minute.' He turned back to the room.

The Doctor smiled at him. 'I am the Doctor,' he said. 'And this is Zoe and Jamie.'

The man studied the trio, his eyes lingering on Zoe again for a moment. 'My name is Roderick Upcott. Normally I'd interrogate you about your unexpected arrival or your outlandish appearance. But with this uprising we've had our hands full.'

The Doctor raised his eyebrows. 'Uprising?'

'Uprising, riot. Call it what you like. We've had all manner of folk streaming into the Concession here, seeking shelter.'

Upcott returned to the window and peered out again through the small opening. 'Quiet as the grave now, though,' he said, closing the shutters and setting his rifle aside. He caught Zoe's eye again and smiled. 'There will be plenty of time for you to tell me your story later.'

'Concession?' said Jamie. 'What sort of place is this? And what's this uprising business?'

'The British Trade Concession in Canton is experiencing some friction with the natives,' said the Doctor blandly. Zoe remembered the glowing string of green script the Doctor had been reading off the screen, and she wondered how much it had told him.

Upcott snorted. 'Friction is a modest way of describing it.' He turned to an ornately carved wardrobe that stood against one wall. 'I had to go out this morning on business. I had a spot of trouble on the way back.' He looked at his ruined shirt for a moment, then he went to the wardrobe and opened its dark wooden door with a screech of rusty hinges. Zoe smelled camphor and lavender and fresh linen in the dark wooden interior.

Upcott reached into the scented recess and took out a folded parcel wrapped in white paper. He closed the door of the wardrobe.

'Just a spot of trouble.' He smiled and untied the ribbon and shook the parcel of white paper open to reveal a clean white shirt. 'One thing I'll say for China, though. It's a good place to get the laundry done.' He removed the pins from the clean shirt, set it carefully aside on one of the wooden chests and began to remove the lacerated rags of the one that still flapped around his ribcage.

As he tugged off the old shirt, Zoe nudged the Doctor. A huge luridly coloured and quite shockingly beautiful tattoo was revealed, curling its sinuous jade-green length from the middle of Upcott's shoulder blades to the centre of his torso. It depicted a dragon breathing flames that curled like flower petals around his navel. He glanced at Zoe, knowing she was looking at the tattoo and amused by her attention. He tossed the ruined shirt aside.

As he did so, something came scampering out of the shadows, its claws scratching across dusty rugs. Zoe gave a little shriek as the small furry shape brushed past her and launched itself at Roderick Upcott, landing nimbly on his back.

Upcott laughed. 'Hello Sydenham.' The tiny black creature cavorted excitedly across his shoulders. 'I was wondering where you'd got to.' The animal chittered in reply, scratching at itself in excitement. Zoe relaxed, now recognising it as a monkey.

Upcott casually scooped the monkey off his shoulder and threw it to one side. The monkey landed nearby, rolling nimbly and regaining its footing with perfect aplomb on the polished wood of one of the long chests.

Upcott pulled on his fresh shirt, covering his tattoo, then scooped up the monkey and returned it to its perch on his shoulder. With the creature riding comfortably, high on his back, he turned to the others.

Jamie was staring at the animal, fascinated by it. The Doctor seemed equally fascinated by the monkey and by Upcott. 'Perhaps we should complete our introductions,' said Upcott.

'That would be nice,' said the Doctor. 'Pray tell us a little more about yourself.'

Upcott smiled. 'Myself? I am a humble merchant. Now, thanks to hard work and the grace of God I've made my fortune trading here in China.' He looked at Zoe. 'And I'm nearly ready to go home.' He went back to the window for a final brief glance into the street. 'I just want to get out with my skin intact.' He closed the shutters and turned back to the door through which they had entered.

Beyond the open door Zoe could see the smoky shapes of the garden. The shifting haze drew back briefly to reveal the TARDIS. But Roderick Upcott wasn't looking at the TARDIS. His attention was elsewhere. Zoe saw that he was staring at the strange stone gateway at the far end of the garden. 'With my skin intact,' repeated Upcott, 'and with a few souvenirs.'

The Doctor had drifted up to join him at the door. 'Tell me Mr Upcott, what do you see as the cause of the current tensions?' The smell of gunpowder wafted to them on a breeze from the garden.

Upcott shrugged evasively. 'Oh, I'd say the Emperor is merely going through one of his periodic fads.'

'Fads?' said Zoe.

'Yes, trying to cast all foreigners out of the Celestial Kingdom. That sort of thing. He has even ordered his Chief Astrologer to do whatever he can.'

The Doctor's eyes brightened with interest. 'Presumably on the supernatural plane.'

'There and elsewhere.'

'What does that mean?' said Jamie. 'The supernatural plane?'

'Magic,' explained the Doctor briefly. He took Roderick Upcott by the arm and led him away, as if for a confidential conversation. Jamie padded over to join Zoe at the door. He peered out into the misty expanse of the garden. 'What's that?' he said, looking towards the stone gates.

'I don't know,' said Zoe. 'There's something odd about it, though. See the way it's built like a gate, but it's got that sort of stone screen thing inside, blocking the entrance. What's the use of a blocked gate?'

On the other side of the room the Doctor was deep in conversation with Roderick Upcott. 'It seems odd,' he was saying, 'that there is such an apparent tang of gunpowder in the air, yet we aren't hearing any sounds.'

Upcott smiled. 'You mean sounds such as gunshots?'

'Or firecrackers going off. Something to create that smell, and that smoke.'

'The smell and the smoke are both the creations of the Imperial Chief Astrologer,' said Upcott. 'The fat little devil's burning a mixture of gunpowder and spices and letting the miasma from this unholy brew spread into the Concession's gardens.' He smiled grimly. 'Sort of an attempt to fumigate us; to smoke out the foreign pest. But we're not having any.' Upcott decisively lowered his rifle, his monkey springing from his shoulder as if following a cue. 'And it's not just the English who are coming in for the treatment.' He smiled indulgently as Sydenham scampered up to him with a long thin cleaning rod clutched in its small simian hands. He took the rod and proceeded to apply it to the barrel of his rifle. 'The Portuguese and other trade nations are all loading their guns and preparing for trouble.'

There was a sudden cry from the door and the Doctor and Upcott turned to see Zoe come running into the room, her face pale. The Doctor hurried to her. 'What is it Zoe? Did you go outside?'

'Just for a moment. Jamie and I. We wanted a closer look at that thing. That gate . . .'

'The spirit gate,' said Roderick Upcott. He finished cleaning his gun and began to reload it with smooth practised skill.

'Oh Doctor . . . Jamie's gone!'

'Gone?' Upcott frowned.

'What is this thing?' murmured the Doctor. 'Show me.'

Zoe led him out into the garden. The smoke was if anything denser now and it had begun to take on an odd pinkish hue. Roderick Upcott followed them out, carrying his rifle. He scowled through the pink haze. 'You see Doctor? The Astrologer's filthy smoke. Comes in fancy colours, too.'

'And it smells odd,' said the Doctor. 'As you said. Not just gunpowder.

Something else. A spice. Ginger? Asafoetida?'

'And opium, I dare say,' murmured Upcott. 'What a waste.'

'This is it,' said Zoe, stopping well short of the black stone gate. It consisted of twin pillars and, set just beyond them, the circular stone screen.

'Curious thing,' said the Doctor. 'What is it?'

Upcott touched the black stone of the nearest pillar. 'As I said, a spirit gate. A traditional Chinese structure, designed to keep demons out.'

'How does it achieve that?'

'Can I interrupt?' said Zoe. 'Jamie has disappeared. This is no time for a discussion of ancient architecture.'

The Doctor flashed her a look that could have meant anything. 'I'm afraid I must disagree. I think this is precisely the time for such a discussion.' He turned to Upcott again.

Upcott shrugged. 'The idea is that demons can only move in a straight line.' He walked, in a straight line, towards the black pillars of the gate.

'No,' said Zoe. 'Don't go in there. That's where Jamie disappeared.'

Upcott didn't even slow down. 'Anyway, that's the Chinese notion.' He strolled briskly between the black pillars and right up to the stone screen beyond them. 'You see, walk in a straight line and you come smack into this.'

The Doctor followed him.

'Doctor, please,' said Zoe. 'Don't go through that gate.'

But the Doctor did, stepping up beside Roderick Upcott. 'I see,' said the Doctor touching the stone screen. 'So the demons run straight into the screen.'

'That's right,' said Upcott. 'And they can go no further. They can't turn corners like us mere mortals.' He turned and walked around the screen and on into the smoky depths of the garden. 'Thus it keeps them out.'

The Doctor also stepped around the screen and followed him. 'I see. While for us it just involves a little detour.' He looked back at Zoe. 'Come on Zoe. It won't do you any harm.'

Zoe remained standing adamantly outside the pillars. 'No. Jamie went through it and disappeared.'

Upcott came looming back out of the pink smoke. 'What did the girl say?'

Zoe frowned at him. 'I said,' said Zoe, 'that Jamie stepped through that thing and vanished. He was there and then he was simply gone.'

Upcott shook his head, smiling a benign patient smile. 'Nonsense, he's merely lost around here somewhere, bumbling around in this smoke.'

But as he said this, a freshening breeze came blowing in and stirred the smoke across the whole length of the garden as if it were a giant hand lifting a sheet. The garden emerged from the haze, clear in every detail, every leaf and stone.

And there was no sign of Jamie.

The Doctor gave Upcott a look of ironic enquiry. 'All right, perhaps he's wandered into one of the Concession buildings. I'll root up some servants to make a proper search of the premises. Would that satisfy your young friend, Doctor?'

'I doubt it,' said the Doctor. 'But well worth a try nonetheless.'

Upcott slung his gun over his shoulder and trotted across the gravel and back into the building. The Doctor turned again to Zoe, who remained stubbornly outside the black stone gates.

'Don't step inside if you don't want to,' said the Doctor coaxingly. 'You might be right. It might indeed be the best course of action.'

For the first time Zoe stirred from the spot where she stood. 'Do you mean that in a sort of a crude reverse-psychology way?'

'No, no. Not at all,' said the Doctor.

Zoe took a hesitant step towards the gate. 'I mean in a sort of Huck Finn painting the fence kind of a way?'

'You mean Tom Sawyer. No, absolutely not,' said the Doctor. 'How do you know about Huck Finn and Tom Sawyer?'

'I did work in a library.' Zoe hovered just outside the black stone pillars. Her voice was tart with exasperation. 'What I'm driving at is that you're trying to get me to come in by telling me to do the opposite.'

'I'm doing nothing of the kind.'

'You think I'm behaving irrationally,' said Zoe. 'But I saw it happen to Jamie. I did.'

'I'm sure you did,' agreed the Doctor hastily. 'And when I say don't step through the gate, I actually and sincerely mean it.'

'He just stepped through it,' said Zoe. 'Like this.' And she stepped forward and through the gate and she was gone. Like the image vanishing from a screen when you switch it off. There was perhaps a slight shimmering of her form as she stepped through the gate, just detectable by the Doctor's unusual eyes.

And then she was gone.

The Doctor sighed. 'Oh dear.' A moment later Roderick Upcott came out of the house and trotted over to him. The Doctor looked at Upcott.

'The servants are just coming. I convinced them that the smoke was gone and the magic of the Emperor's Astrologer had abated.' He looked around and registered Zoe's absence. 'Where's the girl?'

The expression on the Doctor's face answered his question.

'Oh what bad luck,' said Roderick Upcott. 'Losing two in a row like that.'

Chapter Two

Roderick Upcott opened one of the long wooden chests and the smell of high grade opium wafted out. Sydenham watched with keen simian interest. 'Got to watch the little bugger,' said Upcott, of the monkey. 'He'll eat his death in Benares black earth if I let him.'

'Your monkey is addicted to opium?' asked the Doctor, in a non-judgemental tone of voice.

'He will be if I give him half the chance. I try telling him that it's a mortal poison and a spiritual danger but he doesn't pay me any heed.'

'Not surprising,' said the Doctor. 'Patterned verbal communication being rare among the higher primates, except in humans of course.' He smiled and shook his head. 'And I've even met a few of those where it was questionable. Have you tried sign language?'

Upcott reached into the chest. It contained a wooden shelf filled with compartments, each holding a sphere the size of a small cannonball. The spheres were covered with pale dried poppy leaves. Upcott selected one and took it out of the chest.

'Of course he doesn't understand me and it wouldn't do any good if he did. Opium is a cruel goddess who insists on devotion. She is also a deadly poison. A stain on the mortal soul.' Upcott unfolded the blade of a gleaming bronze pocket knife with trembling fingers and began to scrape the dried leaves off the ball. From the streets outside there came the occasional sound of gunfire. Upcott ignored it. 'Nonetheless I feel the need to smoke, after our little adventure in the garden.'

'You weren't even present when it happened,' said the Doctor mildly.

'My God man, how can you be so cold blooded? Your two young companions have just been swallowed by the void.' He used his knife to slice a small piece off the sticky black cannonball.

'Have they?'

'Unless the servants here have failed to find them hiding somewhere among our own buildings. Which I truly doubt.'

'Nonetheless you seem to be taking it rather hard.'

'I hate this heathen sorcery. It gives a man the collywobbles.'

'So you attribute Zoe and Jamie's disappearance to some kind of magical attack by the man who has been wafting the scented gunpowder, the emperor's astrologer?'

'Do you have a better theory?' said Upcott, taking out a long ornate lacquered pipe decorated with red and black triangles. He set it down on a chest and opened a small cherry wood box which contained a tiny, beautifully fashioned spirit lamp.

The Doctor watched Upcott's activity with a frown that might have signified disapproval for the man's obvious addiction to a potentially lethal drug, or any number of other things.

He said, 'Is there nothing more you can tell me about your so-called spirit gate?'

Upcott was now preparing the opium over the spirit lamp prefatory to loading the bowl of his pipe. There was a mad light of anticipation in his eyes as he adjusted the blue flame of the lamp. 'I still can't believe they simply disappeared,' he whispered.

'There's certainly more to your spirit gate than meets the eye.'

'Such as what?' Upcott commenced loading his pipe.

'Such as an ancient teleportation unit drawing on an unknown power source.'

Upcott held the blue flame of the spirit lamp to the tiny lump of opium in his pipe. 'I still say it's the old emperor's magic,' he murmured. The pipe whistled as he smoked.

'Luckily, the energy field around the spirit gate is sufficiently tenacious to draw us in, too,' announced the Doctor, speaking to himself, or perhaps to the living weave of energy that pulsed around him.

He had left Roderick Upcott in the Concession, smoking himself into an opium stupor, and now he stood alone before the control console of the TARDIS.

'All it requires is a few simple modifications.' The Doctor drew aside his soup-stained tie and jabbed a hand into the pocket of his jacket, taking out a small, complex plug board which he quickly and deftly attached to the console, using silver wires taken from a chipped teapot where the spare cables were kept in a fright wig of disorder. 'If I am right and the spirit gate has teleported Jamie and Zoe . . . he mused. He fell silent for a moment, then completed his thought: 'Then we should be able to make use of the teleportation wave and follow.'

The plug board hummed happily and the console experienced a rippling glow of activity. 'That's better. Now we're in business.' The Doctor smiled a distracted smile as his TARDIS came to life around him.

Alive, the vehicle started to vary his location in the universe, shifting him like a joker in a shuffled deck of quantum possibilities. The concepts of 'here' and 'now' began to blur. Certainties dwindled to uncertainties then snuffed out altogether.

Lights flickered in the control room as if threatening to go out permanently and there was a faint smell of burning circuitry. 'Excellent,' said the Doctor and the TARDIS moved with a convulsive shudder.

With a weirdly thrilling surge they were shifted, displaced and then emphatically elsewhere . . .

Chapter Three

The Doctor examined the strange procession of cuneiform figures that danced across the top of the screen. 'England, December 1900 . . . That's interesting.' His brows knotted in a considering frown. 'Precisely a century later . . .'

On the screen the view shifted, showing first a maze of hedgerows, then a rambling mansion standing against a pale winter sky that spread above the snow-shrouded fields of Kent. Looming in the broad white garden, incongruously, stood what looked like the spirit gate from Canton. The Doctor's fingers danced across the console and the spirit gate loomed large on the screen. He studied the markings on it.

'Can it be?' said the Doctor.

'Thomas,' shouted the young woman sitting beside Carnacki, 'What's that thing?'

Carnacki smiled at her as he threw the brake on, easing the Panhard-Levassor to a smooth halt. The 12 horsepower, royal blue automobile was the newest model, imported from France, and had behaved like a dream on this, its maiden voyage from London. Carnacki steered the horseless carriage with aplomb, coming to a halt on the shale driveway outside the huge country house. He glanced back over his shoulder and saw what Celandine had been referring to. The black stone Chinese gate that stood in the middle of the snow covered garden.

'Apparently it's a little souvenir from the Far East brought back by Roderick Upcott in the course of his colourful adventures.'

'Roderick you say?'

'Yes, the late great Roderick. It's his descendant, the distinguished surgeon Pemberton Upcott and his shrewish wife Millicent who are to be our hosts this weekend.'

'Not too shrewish, I hope,' said Celandine, smiling. 'You're painting her a perfect ogre.' She was a plump, pretty blonde with pink cheeks and striking cobalt eyes.

Carnacki smiled back. He was a tall powerfully built young man with a faintly military demeanour. He applied the hand brake, a large lever of an affair, locking the four handmade wheels firmly into place on the icy drive, then climbed out of the car and offered his companion a hand.

'Even if she is, I am sure we'll find some other convivial companions. There'll be plenty of people here.' He looked to the front steps of the house, where a cadre of black clad servants were hurrying out to greet them and smooth their arrival.

He turned back to Celandine, looking charming in her muffler and fur hat in the sharp clean winter air. 'Including the entire Upcott clan. They are compelled to attend this annual Christmas gathering under pain of excommunication. A three line whip, so to speak.'

They watched as the servants took their luggage from the car and bustled back into the house, no doubt in a hurry to get out of the cold. But Carnacki and Celandine were enjoying the winter afternoon and took a turn around the garden, past the austere black shape of the spirit gate. She held his arm as they walked, and their breath fogged in the crisp air.

'Who else can we expect to see this weekend?'

'Besides the Upcotts? Well, the guests this year include Celandine Gilbert, a beautiful young medium who has made something of a smash in smart London circles.'

Celandine smiled at Carnacki as he continued. 'I understand she is to provide entertainment by conducting a séance.'

'With the help of an intense young man known only as Carnacki,' said Celandine, 'who is himself a celebrated student of supernatural phenomena.'

'Hardly celebrated,' muttered Carnacki, his facing going bright red. 'Just getting started really.'

Celandine smiled and changed the subject. 'And who else?'

'Oh, I expect the usual complement of uninvited guests,' said Carnacki, glancing back at the oriental relic. 'You know. Rogues. Unwelcome visitors. Gate crashers.'

The Doctor found it a relatively easy matter to gain access to the Upcott's country house which, as it transpired, was called Fair Destine.

The TARDIS had materialised in a distant corner of the mansion's garden, at the centre of an elaborate hedge maze, now clothed in white and emphatically closed for the winter by a chain that hung at the entrance, its bronze links also clad with snow.

The Doctor had no problem finding his way out of the maze, a trivially easy puzzle with an exit route determined by taking the left turns corresponding to an alternating sequence of primes, starting from the centre of the pattern. But he did get some snow in his shoes and was very glad of the offer of a hot water bottle as he was ushered into the library.

Getting through the front door had also proved a simple enough matter. The butler who had first greeted him had charged up as though accosting an intruder but had quickly slowed as he neared the Doctor and had a better chance to assess the newcomer's status. The Doctor's somewhat dowdy clothing didn't weigh upon the butler at all; he knew a man of substance and authority when he saw one. But he was puzzled.

'Where is your conveyance sir?' he asked.

'Oh I left it back there,' said the Doctor, gesturing vaguely, though truthfully enough, in the direction of the maze, the garden and the distant road.

'And your servants?'

'Around here somewhere I trust. They're always wandering off.'

'Well we'd best get you warm and dry, sir. Come in directly.' The butler, whose name was Elder-Main, guided the Doctor through the shadowy corridors past rooms full of gleaming dark furniture illuminated by the pale snow light from the windows. 'We'll settle you in the library with a nice drop of brandy. Now who shall I say has arrived?'

'The Doctor,' said the Doctor. 'Perhaps you could make that a champagne cognac?'

'Of course sir. I'll tell Mr Pemberton one of his medical gentlemen has turned up and I'll stir out one of the under maids to fetch a hot water bottle, to park the gentleman's feet on while his socks are drying.'

The Doctor waited in the library. He sat in front of an art nouveau fireplace full of blazing logs in the comfortable maroon depths of a sprung old velvet armchair. Every so often he would rise and select a leather bound volume from the shelves and leaf swiftly through it. When he found what he was looking for, he would settle into the armchair, scan the text for a moment or two, then set the volume aside. Finally he returned all the books to their shelves and selected an older and much larger volume. This too was bound in leather, with an odd looking bookmark folded into the centre pages and a large U embossed on the cover. The Doctor glanced at the bookmark, then discarded it and leafed swiftly through the volume, a deep frown on his face. When he finished studying it, he returned it to the shelves and stood looking thoughtfully into space for a moment. 'So,' he murmured. 'The family business, eh?' Then, as if he had come to a decision, he relaxed again. He had just settled back into the chair when he heard footsteps.

The maid came in.

Or, rather, Zoe came in dressed as a maid. She was clutching a large stone hot water bottle with an ivory stopper. 'Where have you been?' she demanded.

'Really, Zoe. There's no need to scold me like that.'

'Well, I was beginning to think you'd never arrive.'

The Doctor opened a silver pocket watch and pursed his lips. 'I thought I'd actually done rather well, but it's hard to say from this.' He held the watch to his ear. 'The poor old thing has stopped.'

'Which makes it extremely accurate, but only twice a day,' sighed Zoe in disgust. 'Now get me out of here. This place is repulsive.'

'Where's Jamie?'

'I have no idea. And believe me, it's not for want of looking. I've been searching for him ever since I arrived here.'

The Doctor inspected Zoe's uniform. 'How did you manage to infiltrate so quickly into the household staff?'

'Infiltrate wasn't in it. They were expecting an additional draft of slaves to handle the Christmas festivities. I saw a column of the poor wretches turning up the driveway and making for the back door of this pile. I realised I could speak the language and it was easy enough to pass myself off as one of them. At least it got me in out of the cold.'

'What did you do about your clothes?' said the Doctor, recalling Zoe's clinging silver one piece jumpsuit. 'I imagine a reflective thermal spacesuit liner would have raised a few eyebrows in the household.'

'It would have if anybody had seen it. I found a coat in the back of one of the cars they parked in a field behind the house. So I pinched it. It covered me up pretty thoroughly and when I got my uniform I hid the suit so none of the others maids saw it. It wasn't easy. They're a nosy bunch. And that room we have to share. You wouldn't believe it. It's tiny. And so cold.'

'Oh, I'd believe it,' said the Doctor. 'By the way, can I have my hot water bottle?' He smiled politely.

'Here,' Zoe shoved it into his hands and turned away.

'I don't mean to be rude,' she added contritely, a moment later. 'But I'm fed up with being one of the serving class. These people expect to be waited on hand and foot and I've had my bottom pinched by at least two miserable gnarly fingered old men.'

'At least two?' said the Doctor with interest.

'The third one might have been a gnarly fingered old woman but it was too dark to make out,' said Zoe. 'And then there's Thor Upcott, Pemberton's younger brother. The word among the servants is to steer well clear of *him*. Can't we just go?'

'Not until we find Jamie. Did you happen to notice the spirit gate in the garden?'

'Notice it? I came through it. It was as if I had stepped through the one in Canton and ended up here.'

The Doctor nodded with approval, as though a theory had been confirmed. 'That explains why the gate appears identical to the one in the Concession garden. It is the same one. But how did it come to be here?'

'It was brought from Canton by that man we met. The one with the tattoo.'

'Roderick Upcott.'

'Yes, as a symbol of his mercantile triumphs or something sad like that. He apparently returned to found a Victorian dynasty and when he died he left them all his immense wealth.' Zoe gestured at the big house that extended around them.

'The wealth that opium brought him.' The Doctor shook his head. 'Poor Roderick. It seems only a moment ago that I left him.' He thought of a figure reclining on a divan in December 1800, wreathed in the smoke of finest Benares black opium which dribbled from a lacquer pipe while the sound of gunfire sporadically spattered around the British Trade Concession.

'Roderick's body is buried in an arboretum attached to the house, a kind of miniature Kew Gardens greenhouse.' Zoe gave a little shudder. 'And Doctor... his pet monkey was buried with him.'

'Yes,' the Doctor nodded. 'The two did seem very attached to each other.'

'Ladies and gentlemen,' said Pemberton Upcott to his assembled guests, 'tonight we will be providing a lecture for your amusement.' Pemberton resembled his great grandfather Roderick in the tobacco colour of his eyes, but there any similarity ended. He was a tall myopic cadaverous man with pebble spectacles and receding silver hair.

He smiled at the crowd sitting around the huge dining table, revealing uneven yellow teeth. 'To be more specific, Mr Carnacki will be providing the lecture and the entertainment.' He nodded to Carnacki, who was seated halfway along the table on his left. Carnacki nodded shyly back, obviously uncomfortable about being singled out at a large social gathering. Pemberton continued relentlessly, apparently unaware of his guest's discomfiture. 'I believe the subject will be the occult, Mr Carnacki?'

'Yes, the occult,' murmured Carnacki. There were appreciative murmurs from the guests. Spiritualism was going through one of its periodic spasms of popularity among the British upper class and was considered a legitimate pastime or amusement, if not a subject for serious enquiry.

Carnacki cleared his throat and spoke up. 'I have brought along the subject of one of my investigations, unearthed several years ago at an archaeological dig in Cornwall. It is of course the "Cornish spirit lance", a medieval jousting weapon, which was the focus of certain horrifying poltergeist phenomena, to be described in my illustrated talk "The Affair of the Spectral Lance".'

There was polite applause from the dinner guests and Carnacki relaxed a little.

Beside him sat Celandine Gilbert. She was holding his hand under the table and could feel his palm sweat at the embarrassment of being singled out, the centre of attention. But the centre of attention moved swiftly on as Pemberton looked at Celandine and said, 'Following Mr Carnacki's no doubt fascinating disquisition we will be entertained by his lovely companion, Miss Gilbert.'

Celandine bowed her head politely as Pemberton went on to describe her career as a medium, at fulsome length. Carnacki leaned close to her and whispered, 'I wish he'd shut up and let us get on with dinner.'

At length their host did just this and, after the meal, a prolonged affair consisting of five courses of which the lobster mayonnaise was an early and unmatched highlight, Carnacki was just about to be led off to the smoking room with the other male guests when a small man in a disreputable jacket came up to him.

'Mr Carnacki,' he said, his eyes gleaming, 'I'm the Doctor. I just wanted to say what a pleasure it is to make your acquaintance at last. I'm a great admirer of yours. You are an extremely brave and resourceful young man dealing with things beyond the capability of most of your contemporaries even to imagine.'

'Why thank you, but – '

'I have followed with fascination the details of your investigations in such matters as the House Among the Laurels, the Whistling Room and the haunting of the *Jarvee*.'

Carnacki stared at the man in mystification. 'I'm afraid I haven't encountered any such cases as you've just described.'

The man smiled, unperturbed, and chuckled to himself. 'No indeed. Not yet.'

'Not yet?'

'Good luck when you do,' said the man, and he patted Carnacki on the shoulder before turning and moving away. Carnacki tried to follow him but the press of the crowd was moving towards the smoking room and he found himself carried along, helpless.

Chapter Four

'It's barbaric,' said Zoe. 'This really is the most primitive culture.' She adjusted the white apron she wore over her black maid's dress and shot an irritated glance at the Doctor. They were standing in a small niche under one of the numerous staircases, safe from observation by unfriendly eyes – the Doctor was a putative guest and guests were not supposed to fraternise too closely with the domestic staff.

'Barbaric in what way, exactly?' asked the Doctor. He seemed genuinely, if rather abstractedly, interested.

'Well for a start after dinner the two sexes separate with the women going off to the drawing room, which at first I thought involved some kind of art classes. You know, sketching or something. But in fact all it seems to entail is a lot of silly prattling and gossip.'

'And no doubt the weaving of subtle feminine stratagems,' said the Doctor. 'As in a coven or seraglio.'

'Meanwhile the men sit around in the smoking room, arguing over what the finest specimens are in the humidor and the correct method of lighting a cigar so they can smoke it and develop exotic carcinomas of the mouth. You can quite see why the women don't want to be in there with them, choking on the smoke. I still don't see why they don't do any drawing, though.'

'The term drawing room is an abbreviation of withdrawing room, so called for obvious reasons.'

'Really? Well I still say that they're a dreadfully primitive lot. And superstitious into the bargain. When they've finished all their smoking and withdrawing that young man called Carnacki is apparently going to entertain them by using something called a magic lantern.'

The Doctor smiled. 'Oh, that's merely a rudimentary kind of slide projector. The name is more affectionate and ironic than anything else. Have you had any luck getting a lead on the whereabouts of Jamie?'

Zoe shook her head. 'No. He's not among the domestic staff. That's for certain.'

'Nor among the guests, at least as far as I have been able to determine.'

'By the way, how did you manage to convince them that you were a guest?'

The Doctor smiled. 'By the simple expedient of asking to wait in the library before my host came to greet me.'

'Yes, that's where I found you. But what's the significance of the library?'

'I correctly surmised that our host, as a distinguished medical man, would keep copies of any papers he had had published. And I was right. While I was waiting for him I managed to read them all.'

'You always were a fast reader,' said Zoe.

'By the time Pemberton Upcott arrived I had acquainted myself thoroughly with his medical career. I was able to converse with him as an equal and discuss a number of technical matters that interested him greatly. So even though I wasn't an officially invited guest I was soon able to convince him that I was a fellow physician and had come with the express purpose of discussing some esoteric questions with a surgeon of genius. That is, himself.'

'In other words you buttered him up. And he bought it?'

'Certainly. He's champing at the bit to sit down and have a proper talk with me.'

'Well, good for you. It's certainly better than pretending to be a downtrodden menial.' Zoe tugged at her apron again, as if it were restricting her entire being. 'You wouldn't like that at all.'

The Doctor shrugged. 'As for Jamie, I hope nothing has happened to him.'

'Well, *something* is bound to have happened to him. After all he's been transported through time and space by that ancient Chinese thingy. That's something enough, isn't it? But I agree with you.' Zoe's voice faltered. 'I hope it's nothing bad.' Suddenly her eyes sparked with interest. 'Wait a minute. Why don't we go out and look at the spirit gate?'

The Doctor shook his head firmly. 'Not just yet. I feel we have had enough trouble with that particular artefact for the time being.'

'But Jamie might be out there in the garden, lost in the cold and snow or something.'

'I think not. I gave the grounds a thorough examination through the screen in the TARDIS. No,' the Doctor peered up into the shadows of the house. 'He's in here somewhere.'

After brandy and cigars and a long and boring discussion about politics, mostly concerning the Kaiser's ambitions and the supreme unlikelihood of a land war in Europe, the gentlemen withdrew from the smoking room and met up with the ladies once again in a broad walnut-floored space called the great lounge. Tall leaded windows looked out across the white expanse of the gardens and in the middle distance the black shape of the spirit gate loomed among swirling clouds of snow.

The great lounge was heated by two log fires burning fiercely in deep walk-in hearths at opposite ends of the room. In the centre of the room, against the inner wall between two symmetrically set doorways was a lustrous grand piano standing in the middle of a red and blue Persian carpet. Celandine caressed its keyboard as she walked past.

'Pity,' she whispered to Carnacki, who was hauling in a lengthy rectangular leather case resembling a rifle bag, but considerably longer and broader in cross section. Carnacki glanced at Celandine and the piano. 'Why? Is it out of tune?'

'No, but it's warm. It's too close to those fireplaces. Heat doesn't do a piano any good.' Carnacki murmured a polite response, but his mind was elsewhere as he prepared the screen for his slide show and opened the brown leather case to reveal the pitted, corroded length of the jousting lance which nestled there among oiled knots of silk.

Carnacki's talk was a considerable success, with even the most obnoxious of the guests finally falling silent and listening with attention as he described one of the oddest occult experiences of his burgeoning investigative career. After some initial nerves, Carnacki's confidence grew, his voice deepened in tone and became firmer and louder. The audience listened, rapt, and Celandine watched him, her eyes glowing with pride.

Also watching with approval from the flickering shadows near the west fireplace was the Doctor, lifting the tails of his jacket to warm his hindquarters as he listened.

When Carnacki finished his account of the occult lance there was prolonged spontaneous applause. Even those sceptics in the crowd who didn't believe a word of the lecture had found themselves engrossed in an enjoyable ghost story. As the lights came up and servants circulated with trays of drinks, Celandine hurried up to Carnacki and handed him a linen handkerchief embroidered with tiny red roses. Carnacki accepted it gratefully and mopped his brow, sighing with relief; he had survived the ordeal. 'Battling the supernatural is one thing,' he told Celandine. 'Public speaking quite another.' He accepted a glass of champagne and swallowed it thirstily.

Among the servants circulating with trays of drinks was the chief butler, Elder-Main. He sidled over and joined the Doctor by the west fireplace.

'Glass of bubbly, sir? Or shall I add a spoonful of sugar and a drop of bitters to make a nice little cocktail for you?'

'Neither, thank you. Tell me, what is that structure attached to the west wing of the house?' The Doctor pointed through the windows where a tall tower could be seen, glazed with snow in the winter moonlight. It had a domed roof and a steel framework with broad panes of glass set between the metal lattices.

'The arboretum, sir. Full of tropical plants and that. Costs a small fortune to heat, especially in the winter. You should hear her ladyship go on about it. But Mr Pemberton is adamant. Cut the heat and all that greenery dies.'

'Isn't that where Roderick Upcott is buried?'

'Very much so sir. Him and his pet chimpanzee, under the spreading mango tree, as our little rhyme goes.'

'Fascinating, although Sydenham was actually a Capuchin monkey. Perhaps I could go and have a look at this grave later?'

'No doubt Mr Pemberton will be providing his guests with a guided tour at some point. It's his pride and joy. But if you want a private visit before that, I dare say something could be arranged.' The butler leaned closer to the Doctor and adopted an intimate, conspiratorial tone. 'And while on the subject of private arrangements, if you cared to spend some more time alone with that little under maid you've taken a shine to, I'm sure we can work something out.'

'Taken a shine to? Oh, you mean Zoe.'

'That's her, sir.' The butler indicated the far side of the room where Zoe was fighting to keep a large tray of champagne glasses stable and upright in the surging crowd of guests.

'I wasn't aware that anyone even knew I'd spoken to her. In fact, I thought we'd taken every possible precaution to remain discreet.'

'Oh, nothing escapes our notice in this house, sir.'

'Evidently not.'

Elder-Main grinned toothily and rubbed his finger against the side of his nose. 'New she is and snooty. But I dare say a few guineas in the right place could loosen her apron strings, so to speak.'

'I see. And you would be looking for a percentage of whatever guineas are involved?'

The butler shrugged modestly. 'Any emolument the gentleman sees fit to send my way sir.'

'Well I'm not sure quite what you mean by loosening apron strings.'

'Of course not, sir.'

'But I'd very much appreciate the chance to speak to the young lady.'

'Naturally. I'll send her over directly.'

Elder-Main was as good as his word and five minutes later Zoe joined the Doctor by the fireplace. 'I imagine you're glad to set that tray down,' he said.

'I certainly am. But whatever did you say to that appalling old butler? He gave me the most gruesome leer when he sent me over to see you.'

'It seems he's made a wild miscalculation about our relationship. But since it's to our advantage there's no point disabusing him.'

'That's what you think. If he leers at me like that again he's going to discover just how much I know about unarmed combat.'

'Tell me, what did you think of our friend Carnacki's lecture?'

'Well he may be your friend but I'm not sure he's mine. If even half of what he says is true I think he's an individual to stay well clear of.'

'Why? Because he's a magnet for strange and dangerous forces?'

Zoe looked at the Doctor, whose face was intermittently thrown into shadow and then illuminated by the red glow of the fire. 'Yes, but then he's not the only one who could be accused of that.' The Doctor's eyes gleamed at her in the flickering light, tiny fires burning in them.

Suddenly the buzz of conversation died away and the big room fell silent around them. 'What is it?' whispered Zoe. 'The next phase of the festivities,' said the Doctor.

Celandine Gilbert was standing on the Persian carpet in front of the grand piano, her eyes shut and her hands clasped in front of her face. As the last mutterings of conversation faded she opened her eyes and said, 'Perhaps some of you have heard of me. In the last few years I've acquired a modest reputation as a medium in England and abroad.'

'Too modest by far,' cried Pemberton Upcott. 'This young lady is the toast of Britain and the continent!' There was a burst of polite applause from the guests but Celandine didn't seem to welcome the interruption, fulsome as it was. She cleared her throat.

'I just wanted to preface this evening's demonstration by saying that my gift is as much a mystery to me as it is to everyone else. I can, to some extent, anticipate when it is going to manifest itself and, to a lesser extent, exert some control over it. But I can never predict exactly what form it is going to take.' She looked around the room with an expression of sober caution. 'Once we begin, anything could happen.'

Listening by the fireplace, the Doctor smiled at Zoe. 'Sounds intriguing, eh?'

'Sounds like the standard huckster's spiel to me,' said Zoe. 'Perhaps afterwards she will start selling us some of her patented snake oil.'

'I think you may have misjudged the young lady,' said the Doctor. 'If her friendship with Carnacki is anything to go by, there is every chance that she is the genuine item.'

'Doctor, come on. A genuine medium? Surely you don't subscribe to any of that spiritualist nonsense? It's the mendacious preying on the gullible.'

'Mostly, but there are some astonishing exceptions. Have you ever heard of Daniel Dunglas Home?' Zoe shook her head. 'Well I must tell you about him,' said the Doctor. 'Or perhaps we should pop in for a visit.'

'Let's just find Jamie and get out of here.'

Before the Doctor could reply, their host began speaking again, addressing Celandine Gilbert. 'Are you sure there isn't anything you need doing? Dim the lights? Have the assembled company join hands?'

'Or pass around the hat so we can fill it with bank notes?' bellowed a red faced man with a wispy tonsure of white hair on his bulging scarlet head.

'Please, Colonel Marlowe,' said Pemberton with a pained expression.

Celandine remained calm. 'No, nothing like that. In fact I prefer to work with the lights fully on.'

'Like D.D. Home,' murmured the Doctor.

'This has the added advantage that there can be no suggestion of fraud,' said Celandine. She gave the Colonel a pointed look.

'Oh, don't mind me dear,' replied the red faced man. 'On with the ectoplasm!'

Celandine ignored him and closed her eyes again. She stood there in the centre of the room, hands clasped at her waist, face pointing towards the floor, in complete silence and concentration. Everyone in the lounge was watching her and a definite tension was developing in the big room. For two full minutes she stood, silent and motionless, and by the third minute the guests were beginning to grow restless. There were coughs, whispers, restless shiftings and a general feeling of a terrible fiasco about to ensue.

Zoe began to feel the same terrible embarrassment that attended witnessing any live performance go horribly wrong. Across the room, Carnacki was watching Celandine with a tense, concerned look. Only the girl herself seemed unconcerned, standing there in front of the piano, pale with concentration.

Pemberton Upcott was wearing the expression of a man who was beginning to wonder if he had made a terrible mistake. He glanced around at his restive guests, came to a decision, and took a step towards Celandine.

It was at that exact moment that the piano began to play, all by itself.

Pemberton froze in mid stride. All muttering and coughing died instantly. Besides the eerie stridency of the piano, the only sound in the lounge was the crackling of the fires. And despite the heat emanating from the two huge hearths, the room suddenly seemed distinctly chilly.

The music emanating from the piano was like nothing any of the guests had ever heard before, a strange stiff-fingered syncopation that nonetheless possessed a lilting, infectious melody.

'Oh listen,' cried the Colonel, drunk and boorish and resolutely unimpressed, 'A squirrel has got into the piano. In fact, a bunch of squirrels. In fact, a bunch of tone deaf squirrels.'

'Be quiet!' hissed a woman standing next to him. 'It's the spirits!'

'Well the spirits need to loosen up their jolly old finger joints and learn some proper music instead of that ugly jungle jabbering!' bellowed the Colonel, delighted at the felicity of his own wit.

But not everyone found the music strange. Zoe had unconsciously begun swaying to the unusual rhythms. 'How odd,' said the Doctor, listening closely. 'Thelonious Monk. 'Crepuscule for Nellie'. There's definitely some kind of temporal displacement afoot.'

The tune came to a plangent conclusion and the piano fell silent. Throughout the incident Celandine had kept her eyes shut and shown no awareness of what was going on. Now, as hesitant applause began among the awed guests she opened her eyes briefly and gestured for silence, returning to her pose of stillness and meditation.

'Well, that was jolly,' bawled the Colonel. 'Shall we break out the port now and let those poor squirrels free?' Several people shot him irritated looks but no one said anything and his comments died strangely in the silent room. Everyone was looking at the piano, expecting it to begin playing again. But when the next incident happened, it took place somewhere else completely.

Along the north wall of the lounge, the wall facing the driveway, there stood a large teak dresser with a display of silver and crystal and a number of candelabra burning on it. It was a heavy slab of furniture and, along with the silverware on top, and presumably inside of it, it must have weighed close to half a ton.

Now the dresser began to move.

At first no one noticed. Then the people standing closest to it realised what was happening and moved hastily away. A woman shrieked. Everyone in the lounge turned to see what was happening and there was a unanimous awestruck gasp from the crowd.

The big teak dresser had risen up off the floor and was now visibly floating six inches above the floor, its stubby feet hovering over the carpet trailing tatters of dusty cobwebs.

'The cleaning staff are in for a severe reprimand,' murmured the Doctor, grinning. Zoe was staring in shock at the dresser. 'How is she doing it, Doctor?' she whispered. The Doctor turned to her, a fierce gleam of interest on his face. 'As I said, she appears to be the genuine article.'

The dresser kept on rising and the crowd had now backed away from the north wall of the lounge, leaving a healthy distance between themselves and the floating dresser. As the press of guests neared the south wall of the room, however, they drew closer to the spot where Celandine stood by the piano and people began to look over their shoulders at the medium and draw back, also leaving a healthy space around her. No one wanted to get too close to Celandine either.

But the Doctor, characteristically, was moving against the flow of the crowd. He set off across the lounge towards the dresser, dragging a reluctant Zoe with him. 'Let's have a closer look.'

'Do we have to?'

As they approached the north wall they found one other person who also wanted to get nearer to the phenomenon. Carnacki. The Doctor smiled and nodded at him, like one connoisseur to another. 'Fascinating, isn't it?' he said. The young man nodded, his face tense.

The dresser had continued to float upwards and it was now about three feet off the floor. But its rate of rise seemed to be faster at one end than the other and the dresser was now slowly tilting, at an angle of about 15 degrees.

'All that silverware and crystal's going to come off with a horrible crash,' said Zoe, who was half wondering if she'd be the one delegated to clear up the ensuing mess.

'I doubt it,' said the Doctor. And indeed none of the objects on the dresser were showing any inclination to shift, not even the big silver plate. 'And notice the candle flames.'

'Ah yes,' breathed Carnacki, a sudden savage grin appearing on his face.

'What do you mean?' demanded Zoe.

The Doctor nodded at the dresser. 'As the candles tilt the flames should remain upright, pointing directly towards the ceiling. But as you can see instead they are tilting along with the candles, perpendicular to the top of the dresser and burning outwards at the same angle.'

'Good God, it's amazing,' said Carnacki. He had a look of triumph, as if Celandine's success was his own.

'It's as if an image of the dresser is being tilted, rather than the dresser itself.'

'Or the laws of physics are in abeyance,' said Zoe.

'Let's get a closer look,' said the Doctor.

'We're already getting a closer look,' complained Zoe. But the Doctor was already moving forward, ducking under the dresser. This was easy enough to do now since the heavy slab of furniture was a good four feet in the air. The Doctor hardly had to crouch to get under it.

'Yes, it's certainly floating,' he reported. 'No doubt about that.'

Zoe remained standing well back but Carnacki ducked under the dresser with the Doctor and took his elbow. 'Best get out from under this thing,' he said. 'It might come down with a crash.' He drew the Doctor out, rather like a parent gently attending to a child, and smiled at him. 'I've seen these demonstrations by Celandine before.'

They turned back to look at the medium, who still stood by the piano, eyes closed, a tranquil expression on her face. Led by Carnacki, they made their way through the crowd towards her. Zoe noticed that the red faced Colonel was standing near Celandine, staring at her; only he wasn't so red faced now. In fact he was looking decidedly pale.

The Doctor had also noticed the man's new demeanour. 'Well, Colonel,' he said. 'Do you think squirrels are also responsible for levitating that dresser?'

The man glanced at them, a look of genuine fear in his eyes, then turned and hurried out through the door on the east side of the fireplace. As he closed the door behind him there a sudden heavy thud on the far side of the room and everyone turned to see that the dresser had returned to earth. 'Extraordinary,' said the Doctor. 'There's not so much a quiver from a single piece of crystal on it.'

Pemberton Upcott came pressing through the crowd to stand beside Carnacki. He was wearing the oddest expression, as though he couldn't decide whether to be terrified by the irrational events he was witnessing or triumphant at the success of his social event. 'Do you think she's finished?' he asked Carnacki. 'Or is there more to come?'

Carnacki shrugged but the Doctor said, 'Oh, I should say there's a great deal more to come.'

As he spoke the windows in the north and west walls abruptly rattled in their frames as if buffeted by an enormous wind. A sharp high keening started outside the house and vast veils of snow blew past, an eerie white in the moonlight. The fires in the twin hearths checked for a moment, dropping back to the embers then rising again in lean columns as if being drawn up the chimneys by a sudden drop in pressure. Then the wind began to shriek with renewed violence and all the window panes rattled. The flow of snow subsided and the winter sky could be seen, dark and glittering with stars.

'Something's going to happen,' said the Doctor. Carnacki nodded. And then there was a guttural surge of thunder in the distance, followed by a white glittering on the far horizon, like distant artillery fire.

A moment later, the thunder came again, this time shockingly close. Then the whole horizon lit up in a band of white fire. The third burst of thunder was even closer; it sounded like a bomb exploding overhead and there were cries of alarm from the guests. Everyone looked up to see the lounge's elaborate crystal chandeliers gently swaying above them.

The next bolt of lightning came down from the sky in a forked surge and struck solidly at the north west corner of the house, striking the domed steel structure of the arboretum. The entire house echoed with the sizzling sound of the electricity and for a moment a blue-white aura surrounded the arboretum. Then it faded and the darkness of the winter night returned.

Celandine Gibson fainted and fell gracefully forward onto the Persian carpet.

Chapter five

'She appears to be in some kind of coma,' announced Pemberton Upcott, turning from the low velvet sofa where Celandine lay, to face the worried Carnacki. They were in the library, which was the nearest room to the lounge that afforded some privacy for the examination of the unconscious girl.

'More like a trance, I'd say.' The Doctor leaned closer to inspect Celandine and then looked up at the other two men. Pemberton tried to conceal his annoyance at being contradicted; he didn't want to show dissension amongst the medical fraternity in front of a layman like Carnacki. 'A mere matter of terminology,' he said. 'In any case, she appears physically sound but deeply unconscious.'

But Carnacki wasn't listening to him. He was looking at the Doctor. 'A trance, you say?' The Doctor nodded. 'As a medium, it is in some ways her natural state,' he said. Carnacki shook his head.

'Trances aren't Celandine's style.' He knelt beside the low sofa and took the girl's hand. She was breathing deeply and quietly, her bosom rising and falling. He put a hand to her forehead. Under her closed lids, her eyes were shimmering with tiny movements, like a dreamer's.

The Doctor left Pemberton Upcott and Carnacki with the unconscious girl and hurried out of the library. Elder-Main was waiting for him in the shadows of the hallway. 'I thought you'd like to know, sir,' he said.

The Doctor looked at him with alert interest. 'Yes?'

'It's the arboretum. You said you were interested in seeing it. Well now might be a good time.'

'I see,' said the Doctor. 'Thank you.' He dug in his pocket and sorted through a fistful of banknotes. 'Let's see, Confederate dollars, Euros, doubloons. Ah. Here we go.' He handed the butler a coin. Elder-Main nodded his thanks.

'And I've told your doxy to meet you there, sir. You can have a bit of privacy if you like.'

'My what? Doxy? Ah . . .' The Doctor smiled and hurried off. Zoe was indeed waiting for him in the arboretum, or rather in the small ante room that intervened between the house proper and the heated confines of the greenhouse. It was a small chamber with square black and white tiles on the floor, floor to ceiling windows on two sides and a revolving door with gleaming brass fittings, such as you might find in a grand hotel, which led into the arboretum. On either side of the door were tall wooden panels carved with blossoming vines.

'Were we really struck by lightning?' said Zoe.

'The house was, at any rate.'

'Do you think it was something to do with the medium and all that business, or was it just a coincidence?'

'Coincidence? No, I don't believe in coincidence,' said the Doctor. 'Celandine's performance may well have triggered something. Now let's investigate the damage.' He moved towards the revolving door.

'Why a revolving door?' said Zoe.

'I suppose it's cheaper than an airlock,' said the Doctor and shoved his way through with Zoe close behind him. The door yielded before them, its glass panels spinning with a whisper on well oiled runners. As they entered the arboretum a welcome flow of warm damp air hit them, lushly scented with the smell of blossoming flowers and green growing things. And something else.

'What's that smell?' said Zoe, wrinkling her nose.

'Ozone,' said the Doctor, looking around him. 'Result of an electrical discharge.'

The arboretum was indeed like a miniature Kew Gardens greenhouse.

Built in the grand tradition of Victorian engineering it rose up, tier after tier of glass in a solid matrix of thin steel girders. Arrayed throughout the structure was every imaginable kind of tropical blossom, creeper, fern, shrub and orchid. Several full grown trees bore a lush burden of ripe fruit. Zoe could see the yellow of lemons and the polished green of limes. Just ahead of them, around a curve of the greenhouse, she could see the hanging branches of a tall tree bearing larger, less familiar fruit.

'What are those?'

'Mangoes,' said the Doctor. Then he quoted, '"Him and his pet chimpanzee, under the spreading mango tree".' He hurried ahead and Zoe followed. 'Or at least they were,' said the Doctor.

By the roots of the mango tree was what had once been the only unplanted patch of earth in the entire arboretum. Above the square segment was a rectangular headstone of white marble seamed with pink. Angular black lettering set into the marble read RODERICK UPCOTT AND HIS BELOVED PET SYDENHAM. Below this were two sets of dates; in the monkey's case, recording a pathetically brief life span. Among the lush plantings of the greenhouse, in the shade of the mango tree, it was an altogether picturesque and peaceful place for a grave.

Except there was no grave. Not any more. Just a raw wound in the loam, like the crater left by a small explosion. The Doctor was examining this with fascination. 'Incredible,' he murmured, lifting one leg to climb into the hole.

'Doctor!' Zoe grabbed his jacket and pulled him back. 'It's a grave.'

'It was,' said the Doctor, taking out a pair of what looked like spectacles with thick circular black metal frames. 'There's no body in there any more. See for yourself.'

Zoe peered into the pit. It did indeed appear to be empty. The Doctor had placed the spectacles on his nose and was peering through them as they buzzed and their lenses changed colour, cycling from yellow to deep indigo.

'What are you doing?'

'Checking for the telltale signature of certain gases. Don't ask what sort.'

'What sort?'

'The kind usually associated with the decay of a human cadaver.'

'Oh.' Zoe fell silent and watched as the Doctor peered around the arboretum with his spectacles buzzing and changing colour. 'What do they tell you?'

'Nothing,' said the Doctor. He took the spectacles off and returned them to a small sequinned case, which he stored in a pocket. 'That is, they tell me that there is no trace of any such gases.'

'And what does that mean?'

'That Roderick Upcott's body isn't lying around here anywhere.'

'Ugh, I should hope not. Do you think the lightning bolt destroyed it?'

The Doctor crouched by the hole again. 'If so, it must have been very thoroughly vaporised.' He touched the sides of the hole where the dirt had a strange sheen. 'Is it still warm?' said Zoe.

'More than that,' said the Doctor. 'It's smooth. It's been turned to glass. So extraordinary temperatures must have been achieved.'

'Not surprising if it was on the receiving end of a lightning bolt.'

'No,' agreed the Doctor.

'So Upcott's body could have been completely vaporised.'

'I suppose. Along with that of the faithful simian Sydenham.' The Doctor didn't seem convinced. He glanced around suddenly. 'Do you feel that?'

'What? That cool breeze?'

'Yes. Not exactly the sort of thing that's encouraged in a greenhouse. Where is it coming from?' He looked up. Zoe followed his gaze and saw that there was a ragged tear in the fabric of the building high above them. An irregular oval hole had been made on the north side of the tower, framed by a twisted loop of steel and spattered with gleaming nacreous clots of melted glass.

'That's where the lightning bolt came in.'

'Yes indeed,' murmured the Doctor. He stood up and looked at the hole in the ceiling and back down at the crater beneath the mango tree.

He said, 'It's all a bit neat, don't you think?'

Just then there was the sound of the revolving door swishing somewhere beyond the immediate curtain of green foliage. The Doctor and Zoe both turned around; someone was coming into the arboretum. A moment later they heard footsteps and Carnacki appeared, a deep groove of worry dividing his young forehead. 'I was told I might find you here.'

'What's wrong?' said the Doctor. 'Is it Celandine?'

'No. She's all right. Or at least her condition remains as it was. Some kind of deep coma or trance. But I'm afraid something else is wrong.' He looked at them. 'I don't quite know how to put this, but there's been a murder.'

Chapter Six

Pemberton Upcott and his wife Millicent were waiting outside the billiard room when Carnacki approached, with the Doctor and Zoe following close behind. Pemberton moved forward to greet them, but his wife intervened, putting herself in front of him and intercepting the newcomers.

'Mr Carnacki, we are so pleased you could help.' She was a tall nervous woman with a thin lined face that had once been beautiful. She seemed to be seething with some kind of internal rage. Her eyes were smoke grey and appeared to alternate between inattention and fury, although at the moment they chiefly registered fear. She tried to smile, revealing small white teeth, and glanced back towards the source of her fear, the billiard room. Her husband stepped forward.

'We were hoping – '

But his wife cut him off. 'We were hoping Mr Carnacki that you could do everything in your power to try to help us resolve this unfortunate situation. We know that you are an investigator of criminal matters.'

Carnacki nodded, impatient and nervous. 'You must realise that my status as an investigator of criminal – and other – matters is purely unofficial. And I'm not sure how amenable this situation is to any final resolution. But within those boundaries, yes, of course. I'll do my best to help.'

Mrs Upcott's eyelids dipped momentarily with relief. She flashed Carnacki a smile of gratitude and stood aside to let her husband take over – now that the important matters had been settled.

Pemberton seemed unabashed at having to operate in the shadow of his wife. He was evidently well used to it, even resigned to it, unusual as that might seem among the almighty male-dominated society of England in 1900.

Although maybe it wasn't so unusual, reflected Zoe. Throughout human history there had been no shortage of public tyrants who were privately henpecked.

Pemberton Upcott had seized Carnacki's hand and was vigorously shaking it. 'Thank you old fellow. I was hoping I might count on you, and your discretion.'

'Of course,' said Carnacki in a non-committal tone. The discretion was a new factor.

'The room has been left much as it was when we found it. We assumed you would want to look around.'

'Yes, perfect.' Carnacki looked towards the closed door of the billiard room, which by now could not have assumed a more sinister aspect if there had been blood seeping under it in a steady flow. The Doctor and Zoe exchanged a look. Zoe silently mouthed a question: *What is it?* In reply, the Doctor merely shrugged.

'So please go ahead,' said Pemberton Upcott, beginning to move towards the door. 'Although perhaps I can accompany you and provide some assistance?'

Pemberton's wife, who had been standing silently in the shadows, both figuratively and literally, for the past few moments now stepped forward again. She took her husband firmly by the arm, restraining him. 'We ought to leave Mr Carnacki as free a hand as possible, wouldn't you agree, dear?'

For an instant Pemberton flushed with something that might have been anger, then he regained his calm. 'Of course, dear.' He stood back and gestured towards the door of the billiard room. 'It's all yours, Mr Carnacki. I will just show you in and explain how we came to find, er, it.' He glanced at his wife. 'Then I'll leave you alone. You shall have an entirely free hand.'

'Although if you require any help from any of the servants, you have only to ask,' said Mrs Upcott, interrupting and undercutting her husband's authority in a highly effective fashion.

Carnacki shook his head. 'I only ask that you allow me to, as it were, deputise the Doctor, whom I believe even on our short acquaintance will prove to be of invaluable assistance in my enquiries. An effective Watson to my Holmes, or perhaps even a Holmes to my Watson.'

'Of course,' said Pemberton. But it was his wife who gave the Doctor a shrewd measuring look that didn't entirely signify approval. Mrs Upcott was encountering a creature outside her experience and she knew it and didn't like it.

The Doctor smiled toothily and said, 'And I in turn would like to ask your kindness in allowing us to borrow one of your domestics. Zoe here.'

Pemberton Upcott and his wife nodded, not wasting words on Zoe, and Mrs Upcott looked through her as if she were not there as she walked away down the corridor, her feet scuffing down the corridor on the thick carpet.

Pemberton unlocked the door of the billiard room and they went inside, Zoe feeling a liquid fluttering in her stomach as she stepped over the threshold.

The billiard room was, by the standards of Fair Destine, small and cosy. About thirty feet by twenty, it was a windowless wood panelled affair with wall to wall green carpet that echoed exactly the colour of the felt on the long, elegant billiard table that occupied the centre of the room. There was a trio of ceiling lamps hanging over the table, three large milky glass discs, each several feet across, which provided clear illumination for the players. There were no players at the moment; the room was apparently completely unoccupied. At the far end there stood a pair of floral armchairs on either side of a small black card table draped with linen, with an unopened deck of playing cards on it, invitingly ready for a game. A tall standard lamp stood behind the table, its central column fashioned of ornate gilded metal, its shade a square box of green fabric hung with long tassels of the kind that also concealed the legs of the chairs and the table. Zoe recalled that the Victorians had had a thing about bare legs, even the legs of furniture.

At the other end of the room, near Zoe, there was another table and lamp, accompanied by a single armchair. The table here was covered with an assortment of crystal decanters with tarnished silver stoppers. In the crystal depths of each container gleamed an amber liquid more inviting to some than the playing cards.

Pemberton Upcott moved towards this chair, stepping around the billiard table as he did so. For the first time Zoe noticed that the tip of a man's shoe could be seen on the floor on the far side of the table. Her stomach turned over and she looked away as the Doctor and Carnacki crowded eagerly around the billiard table to join Pemberton.

'This is exactly how we found him. We – '

The Doctor interrupted Pemberton. 'I noticed that when you opened the door the lock was broken.'

Pemberton looked at the Doctor, perhaps taking full account of him for the first time. 'Yes. We had to force the door to get in. But we did so judiciously and, I thought, expertly. I'm surprised you noticed anything.'

'Why did you force the door?' said Carnacki.

Pemberton suppressed his irritation. 'It was locked from the inside. And only the Colonel had a key.'

For the first time Zoe made herself look down, and saw the man from the lounge sprawled there on the floor. The red faced man who had so mercilessly heckled Celandine Gibson in the course of her séance. He wasn't so red faced now.

'There was only one key to the billiard room?' persisted Carnacki.

'Yes, it's sort of my private retreat. I don't even let my brother in here, much less anyone else.'

'What happens if a guest wants a game of billiards?' said the Doctor. Pemberton looked at him with exasperation. 'Then they just have to make do with one of the tables in the smoking room.'

Poor guests, thought Zoe.

'So there's just the one key,' concluded Pemberton.

'Yet you lent it to the Colonel,' said Carnacki, speaking for the first time since they had entered the room.

'The Colonel was my uncle,' said Pemberton, looking down at the body. He said this with an air of finality, as if it explained everything. But Carnacki apparently wasn't satisfied.

'Why were you so helpful?' he said.

'What do you mean? He was my uncle.' Pemberton looked at Carnacki with barely concealed anger.

Carnacki was unperturbed. 'Yes, but uncle or not, he had offended you.'

'What do you mean? Who says that?'

The Doctor intervened. 'No one says it. But it was perfectly obvious to anyone who was present in the lounge during Miss Gibson's performance. You were dreadfully embarrassed by his loud remarks.'

Zoe looked at Pemberton Upcott in a new way. He suddenly looked like a potential murderer.

'Remarks,' added Carnacki, 'that were boorish and antagonistic in the extreme.' He looked at the man lying on the carpet. 'While not wishing to speak badly of the dead, the Colonel's behaviour was ill mannered and unforgivable.' He looked at Pemberton Upcott with a cold light in his eyes. 'And he was behaving this way on an occasion where you had gone to a great deal of trouble to arrange an entertainment for your guests. An occasion that meant a great deal to you, one where you might say you felt your honour, or at least your self esteem, was at stake. And here was the Colonel, trying to spoil everything.'

The Doctor shook his head and added, 'I seem to remember some particularly unfortunate remarks about squirrels.'

Pemberton looked down at the body on the floor then back up at the others. When he spoke, he seemed genuinely sad and for the first time Zoe had a sense of the man as a real human being with feelings.

'Uncle was outspoken and something of a fool, it's true. But he wasn't a bad old skin. And while I was furious with him for making a display of himself, I had some understanding of what motivated his remarks.'

'What could motivate such rudeness?' said Carnacki, stepping towards the drinks table and looking at a brandy snifter that sat there, with an inch of amber spirit still in it. He looked at Pemberton. 'Besides strong drink I mean.'

'My uncle wasn't drunk. At least not by his standards. No, it was fear rather than intoxication that caused him to behave like that.'

'Fear?' said Zoe.

'Fear of the supernatural,' said the Doctor.

Pemberton gave him a sharp look. 'That's right. My uncle had a life long dread of anything to do with the occult or the unknown. How did you know that?'

'By his remarks in front of the medium. Why else should a man be so abusive to a young woman, unless he feared what she might reveal to him?' The Doctor crouched beside the dead man. 'Isn't that right, Colonel?' Then the Doctor looked up at the others. 'And he fled from the room, as soon as evidence of Miss Gibson's powers became impossible to ignore. That confirmed my assessment of him.'

All the talk of drink seemed to have made Pemberton thirsty. He moved to the table and poured a measure from the cognac decanter. 'It's true. He was very shaken by the séance.'

'A man who was forced to reappraise his beliefs,' said Carnacki. 'A man therefore in great spiritual distress.'

Pemberton nodded. 'He wanted to be left alone. To have a drink to steady his nerves.' Pemberton sipped his own brandy. 'So I lent him the key to my billiard room. It seemed the best place. And after half an hour I went to see how he was . . .'

'And the door was locked and there was no reply,' said Carnacki.

'Yes, so I began to get worried about the old fellow. And finally I forced the door, or had it forced, and found him like this.'

'Exactly like this?' said Carnacki.

'The room has been restored to exactly the way we found it.'

'You didn't move the body?'

'Yes I did, of course I did. To make sure that he was . . . gone. But I restored it to its former position, as nearly as I could.'

Carnacki nodded, satisfied. 'What makes you think it wasn't natural causes?'

'This,' muttered Pemberton. He rolled the body over to reveal that the Colonel had acquired what looked like the tattoo of a miniature red dragon in the centre of his forehead.

'Hmm, yes, that does seem fairly unequivocal,' said the Doctor.

'So that's as much as I know,' said Pemberton. 'Now I am available if you should need anything, but otherwise I'll leave you to your investigation.' He turned and went out, closing the door behind him.

Crouching by the body, Carnacki rose to his feet again and began to pace the length of the carpet. The Doctor went and looked at the body again, then up at Zoe. 'Colonel Red in the Billiard Room,' he said quietly.

Carnacki stopped pacing and gave a sharp frown of puzzlement. 'I thought his name was Marlowe.'

The Doctor smiled. 'Forgive me. I was just thinking of something else.'

'I know what you mean though, Doctor.' said Zoe. 'It is like a classic murder mystery.'

'I don't see what's so classic about it,' said Carnacki. He bent over the body and took a leather case from the pocket of his tweed jacket. From this he drew a magnifying glass. 'It's brutal and sordid and terribly commonplace.' He held the magnifying glass over the tattoo of the red dragon. 'Except for this.'

'It's a clue,' said Zoe drily.

'I hate to sound so conventional,' said the Doctor, 'but maybe the best thing for us to do is simply to send for the police.'

Zoe shook her head. 'No chance, I'm afraid. The blizzard has cut us off. And the telephone is out of order, which is hardly surprising considering the lightning strike and the primitive state of the equipment in the first place.'

Carnacki smiled wanly. 'Primitive state?' He looked up at Zoe. 'The Post Office wouldn't like to hear that, Miss.' He turned away from the body with a sense of relief, as though he'd discharged an unpleasant duty. His smile brightened and Zoe realised that he was an attractive man. 'You ought to be asking awkward questions like that in Parliament. Are you a suffragette by any chance?'

'I'm well beyond being a suffragette,' said Zoe.

'By the way,' said the Doctor. 'How did you glean all this information? About the telephone and so on?'

'I heard the servants talking.'

Carnacki peered at her thoughtfully. 'You say that as if you're not a servant yourself.' Zoe felt her cheeks reddening. She felt she'd been caught out in her imposture.

The Doctor intervened. 'Zoe is my travelling companion. Circumstances have compelled her to pass incognito in this household.'

Carnacki seemed to accept this. He took another leather case from another tweed pocket and unfolded it to reveal a yellow linen tape measure. 'I believe I shall take some measurements.'

'Excellent idea,' said the Doctor.

Carnacki kneeled on the floor while Zoe and the Doctor wandered to the opposite end of the room for a confidential conference. 'Doctor,' murmured Zoe, 'that dragon . . .'

'I know. It's strikingly similar to the one we saw tattooed on Roderick Upcott.'

'About a hundred years ago.'

'Exactly a hundred years ago.' He glanced back at the corpse.

'Except Roderick's dragon was green and this one is red.'

The Doctor frowned thoughtfully. 'Which is to say, its spectral opposite in terms of colour. I wonder if that's significant?'

Carnacki came and joined them, jotting measurements down in a small blue notebook. 'That's about all I can do until I get the camera in here.'

After Carnacki had taken his photographs and completed all kinds of measurements, which seemed to Zoe to take forever, with the Doctor watching and nodding and occasionally interfering with things, the first faint light of dawn was showing through the windows.

Carnacki put the notebook in his pocket. He seemed only a little wearied by his night of exertion. And the Doctor of course was disgustingly chipper. 'Now if you don't mind,' said Carnacki. 'I want to go and see if Celandine has recovered consciousness.'

'Of course,' said the Doctor. 'What is it?'

This last was addressed to Elder-Main, the butler, who was standing in the open door of the billiard room. The man had a shocked, ragged look on his face which amply justified the urgency of the Doctor's question.

Elder-Main looked down at the body on the floor for a moment, then hesitantly up at them. 'It's Mr Pemberton sir. He asks if you can come immediately.'

He cleared his throat. 'There's been another one.'

Chapter Seven

The Doctor blew on the hot dark tea in his cup. He said, '"Another one" transpires to be Pemberton Upcott's elderly Aunt Arabelle, who was found in her bed this morning by the servants.'

'A bit early wasn't it? Even for servants,' said Zoe.

'The lady was in the habit of rising early and she could by no means dress herself.'

'Why, was she paralysed?'

'Only with wealth,' said the Doctor. He was sipping tea with Zoe in the breakfast room, a pleasant red tiled alcove adjacent to the kitchen, warmed by a large pale yellow enamelled wood burning oven. Zoe had been furious to note that over the door there was a servant summoning device. It consisted of a bell with a pull rope and a black iron arrow which rode along a short length of black iron rail to stop at any one of a sequence of hand written cards, indicating the title of the unfortunate underling.

The Doctor was sipping tea while Zoe poured it. 'This really is ridiculous,' she said. The Doctor looked up from his cup and peered at her judiciously. 'The murders?'

'No. This.' She indicated the starched white apron that she wore fastened so tightly around her shapeless black dress. 'This whole servant business. Why can't I just get out of these ridiculous clothes and this ridiculous role and . . .'

'And?'

'And sit drinking tea with you for a start instead of having to serve it.'

'Oh dear, of course. Sit down,' said the Doctor, fussing with dusting off a chair with his handkerchief. 'Let me get you a cup.'

'No,' snarled Zoe. 'That's not what I mean. I don't want to sneak a cup of tea with you and have to leap to my feet if someone comes in and start behaving like a servant. Why can't we just upgrade my status? Tell people that I'm your friend so they can stop treating me like some lower form of life.' She hooked a finger in her collar and tugged at the starched material. 'And I can get out of this potato sack.'

The Doctor got up and went to Zoe. He spoke to her quietly and intimately. 'I appreciate the discomfort you're tolerating, Zoe. Both physical and social. But if we can continue with your charade just a little longer it may enable us to learn something about the events that are taking place in this house. Not only the murders but Jamie's disappearance.'

'How could I possibly achieve that by pretending to be a dreadful little skivvy?'

'Because people will allow you to see and hear things as a maid that they would never permit if you were a social equal.'

'I suppose,' said Zoe. 'I suppose you have a point.'

The Doctor smiled. 'So you will remain a maid a little longer?'

'Unless I get murdered,' said Zoe darkly.

'Don't even joke about that,' said the Doctor.

'But it might happen, mightn't it?'

The Doctor peered out of the narrow window on the whitewashed wall adjacent to the pantry door. Outside, a pale winter sun could be seen edging up over the snow covered garden. 'Whatever is responsible for these killings, I have a feeling it won't operate by daylight.'

'But the old lady was killed this morning.'

'Her body was found this morning, just after dawn. We can surmise that she died sometime before that.'

'And they're sure she didn't just pass away in her sleep? Of old age?'

The Doctor shook his head emphatically. 'No.'

'She had another one of those dragon tattoos on her forehead?'

'Yes,' said the Doctor. 'Although I'm not sure they're tattoos. In fact, I'm not at all sure what they are. Ah. Toast.'

'What?' said Zoe. But then a moment later she could smell it too. A warm aroma of freshly toasted bread, which stirred the digestive juices in an agreeable fashion. The Doctor had detected it while it was just the faintest stirring on the air currents. He had a very keen nose.

Carnacki came in, carrying a large silver toast rack containing half a dozen slices of golden brown bread. In the crook of his arm he awkwardly balanced a saucer of butter, a jar of thick red jam and a small pot of honey.

'Here let me help you,' said Zoe, moving to take something before he dropped everything. But Carnacki dodged around her. 'No,' he said, smiling. 'Let me wait on you.' He had been deferential to Zoe in an amused and mildly annoying avuncular fashion ever since she had delivered what he referred to as her 'suffragette's manifesto' in the billiard room. It seemed that Carnacki was a champion of women's rights, at least in an archaic, naïve and offensively condescending fashion. Zoe cut him a little slack, though. After all, he was a creature of his time.

Carnacki put the toast and condiments down on the big oak slab of table and smiled at Zoe and the Doctor, taking a knife and spoon out of the pocket of his tweed jacket. Zoe made a mental note not to use that knife or spoon. 'So Celandine is improving?' said the Doctor.

Carnacki paused, startled. 'How did you know that?'

'By your smile,' said Zoe.

Carnacki smiled bashfully and shrugged. 'I suppose I am one of those people whose soul can be read in his face.'

'There's nothing wrong with that,' said Zoe.

'Just don't try playing poker,' said the Doctor, reaching for the toast rack.

'In any case Celandine is still unconscious.' Carnacki buttered his toast. Zoe glanced quickly at the Doctor. Surely it was a bad sign for someone to remain unconscious for so long? The Doctor gave her a bland look and turned to Carnacki.

'How can we construe that as good news?'

'Because her colour is better, her breathing deeper and more regular, but most crucially she has begun to talk.' Carnacki picked up the jam jar and began spooning jam onto his toast. 'Or at least to mutter broken phrases. Nothing anybody can quite make out. But surely the ability to speak is a good thing in itself, indicating as it does a less profound coma or trance, a shallower state of unconsciousness.'

The Doctor pursed his lips. 'I'd say so, yes.'

Zoe poured the tea.

'So Doctor. What do we make of these killings?'

'I was just about to ask you the same thing,' the Doctor was suddenly serious. 'Considering that you're an expert in your field it would be foolish not to take advantage of your expertise.'

'Well, that's the question, isn't it?' Carnacki bit off a mouthful of toast, chewed politely and at maddening length and finally said, 'The question is whether these killings fall into what you call my "field". That is, the occult, the supernatural, the unexplained.'

'And do you think they do?' said the Doctor.

Carnacki gnawed away at his toast, nodding enthusiastically. 'I think one would have to be a pretty dull chap to be shown that unearthed and empty grave in the arboretum – exhumed by lightning! – and not combine it with the subsequent, or contemporaneous, murders.' He chewed and swallowed and smiled. 'Putting two and two together.'

The Doctor was looking across the table at Carnacki with fixed intensity. 'And coming to what result?'

'The revenant of Roderick Upcott himself . . . '

'The what?' said Zoe.

'Ghost,' said the Doctor.

'Or, at the very least, his reanimated cadaver,' added Carnacki, reaching for another piece of toast. 'Which is responsible for the murders, ghoulishly stalking the corridors of Fair Destine on a remorseless lethal mission.'

Zoe glanced at the Doctor. 'He presents a persuasive case.'

'Do I detect a note of sarcasm?' Suddenly Carnacki was looking directly at Zoe and the cool intelligence of his eyes immediately dispelled any image of a toast chomping buffoon.

'Yes, well I suppose so, I'm sorry.'

The Doctor interrupted smoothly. 'Zoe hasn't had quite your level of experience with the occult and outré, Mr Carnacki. She's entitled to a little sardonic scepticism.' He turned to Zoe and said, with a gentle note of reproof, 'But Mr Carnacki knows whereof he speaks.'

'And you're inclined to agree with him?'

The Doctor shook his head and smiled at Carnacki. 'I'm afraid not. I don't think things can be quite so straightforward.'

'Straightforward?' said Zoe in a scandalised tone.

There was a ringing noise from above the door and the Doctor looked up at the servant-signalling device over the door. He read the card indicated by the black iron arrow.

'Under maid. Zoe, isn't that you?'

Arabelle Daphne Upcott stared up at the ceiling of her bedroom, her dead eyes unseeing. The Doctor stared down at those unseeing pupils with compassion and accepted a small sealed bottle and a white cloth from Carnacki. The bottle contained methyl alcohol. The Doctor dabbed some on the rag and gently applied it to the old woman's forehead, where the livid red tattoo of the dragon flared.

'Nothing?' said Carnacki.

'It certainly doesn't appear to be coming off,' said the Doctor. He examined the unblemished white rag and then turned his gaze to the tiny red dragon, dancing rampant in triumph on the dead woman's forehead. 'I still don't believe it's a tattoo, although I must confess I don't have a better explanation. At least not yet.' He moved away from the bed and gave Carnacki room to get his camera in; it was a huge affair on a tripod that stood almost as tall as the Doctor.

Carnacki ducked inside the camera's hood and framed the scene. Arabelle Upcott's body was lying where it had been found, in a wide feather bed, a four poster in her bedroom in the west corner of the house, overlooking the arboretum.

As with Colonel Marlowe in the billiard room, the Doctor and Carnacki had instructed that the murder scene should be left exactly as it was found. A fond hope with the number of servants, family members, and salaciously nosy guests who had tramped through by now. But at least the bodies remained *in situ*, with the Doctor's sensible suggestion that no fires be lighted in either room, to keep things as cool as possible.

Carnacki emerged from under the camera's black shroud. His breath fogged on the chilled air of the room. 'It's as cold as a crypt,' he said. The Doctor nodded. Carnacki fussed with his camera, ducked back under the hood and suddenly there was a flash of magnesium and the poor woman's face was for an instant whiter still.

As the flash dissipated, the Doctor turned to see that someone was standing in the doorway of the bedroom. It was Pemberton Upcott. 'Are you quite finished with the remains of my aunt?' he said savagely.

Carnacki emerged from under the hood of the camera. 'Of course,' he said. He was making allowances for his host's bad temper. The man had suffered two bereavements and he had been up all night under great strain.

Carnacki too had been up all night, but he was riding high on a fast flowing tide of adrenaline and Indian tea. It was always like this when an investigation was under way. He would hardly pause for sleep or sustenance.

He began to pack up his camera discreetly as Pemberton stood staring stonily down at the body of his aunt. Meanwhile the Doctor was at the door, in private conversation with the chief butler, Elder-Main, who had followed his master into the room like his shadow.

The Doctor came over and joined Pemberton by the bed.

'Mr Upcott, was your aunt related to you by blood or by marriage?'

Pemberton didn't look at the Doctor. His gazed remained fixed on the unfortunate woman on the bed. 'What does that have to do with anything?' he said.

'Please.'

'She was my father's sister,' snarled Pemberton. 'And my last living aunt. Why?'

'And the recently deceased Colonel Marlowe. Was he the brother of your father or your mother?'

Pemberton suddenly turned and faced the Doctor. 'I don't understand why you are prying into my life with these highly personal questions. I find them both annoying and highly distasteful.' He turned on his heels and strode towards the door where the Butler waited. But before they could leave, the Doctor spoke again. 'Mr Upcott, I thought you had agreed to help us in this investigation in whatever way you could.'

Pemberton and the butler paused on the threshold. 'Well, what is it you want to ask me?' said Pemberton impatiently.

The Doctor smiled politely. 'Just one final question: I believe you had the lock repaired on the billiard room door?'

'Yes, I thought it was by far the most sensible thing to do. Stop people traipsing in and out. The lock was made good and the door sealed again, but nothing inside the room was disturbed. What of it?'

'My question is, did you change the lock or merely repair it? In other words, is there a new key in use?' The Doctor peered keenly at Pemberton. 'Or perhaps more than one?'

'No, just this one, which is unique,' said Pemberton impatiently. 'As I have told you.' He reached into his watch pocket and took out the key, which he brandished defiantly. 'And here it is.'

'Fine. Thank you.' The Doctor watched Upcott and the butler go, then he turned to Carnacki who was looking at him with a puzzled expression.

'What was all that about Doctor?'

'It seems there have been developments in our murder investigation.'

'You've discovered some significant fact?'

'Yes, it seems Pemberton is wrong about there being only the one key.'

'Really? How can we be sure of that?'

'Did you see me talking to the butler a moment ago?'

'Yes, I could hardly miss it.'

'Well he passed me a message from Zoe. Do you remember when she was summoned from the breakfast room by that contraption? Well her summoner was Pemberton's brother.'

'Thor Upcott.'

'Yes. And it seems Thor summoned her from the supposedly locked and impenetrable billiard room, where she found him sitting drunk as a lord. He ordered some scrambled eggs.'

'These eggs aren't at all bad,' said Thor Upcott, stirring them on the small china plate with his fork, a tufted heap of buttery golden eggs streaked with pink slivers of smoked salmon.

'That's good,' said Zoe nervously.

'For a while we had this lamentable cook who insisted on using the most revolting over-salted Scotch salmon. We got rid of him pretty quick, I can tell you.' Thor bent to the eggs and shovelled them into his mouth with astounding rapidity. Then, setting the plate aside, he turned to Zoe.

Zoe had found Thor Upcott in the billiard room where he'd ordered breakfast from her, insisting that she bring it to him in his bedroom.

Once she'd arrived, he'd insisted on her remaining there while he ate. It was a large room at the east end of the house with south facing windows. There was a bed at one end and a low sofa at the other. The walls were lined with bookshelves. A dresser with a marble top occupied most of the length of the north wall with a large mirror mounted behind it, doubling the images of bottles of eau de cologne and other toiletries chaotically mingled with larger bottles of whisky and brandy, and a soda siphon.

Thor had been drunk when she first found him, but he seemed to have sobered up rapidly since leaving the billiard room. Zoe didn't feel any more at ease with him, though. In fact she felt as if she were trapped in a cage with a huge prowling panther.

Thor Upcott was a larger and more athletic version of his brother. He had a powerful build, which put Zoe in mind of his ancestor Roderick. Thor had broad shoulders and a narrow waist, which he showed off to good advantage in the clinging silk dressing gown he wore. Zoe suspected he wasn't wearing anything else, except his faintly ludicrous slippers. The robe was figured with a geometrical pattern in brown, yellow and green. It had truncated, gaping sleeves which revealed the man's powerful arms, which terminated in oddly small, almost feminine hands. Thor's face bore a close resemblance to his older brother's, but whereas Pemberton's countenance was deeply scored with lines of anxiety Thor's was unmarked and almost childlike; the face of a man who had no worries.

Thor turned to the dresser and took a cigarette from a cylindrical pewter case in a pale brown pigskin cover. As he lit the cigarette Zoe scooped up his breakfast plate and quickly headed for the door.

'What are you doing?' Thor blew a lazy smoke ring. 'Put that bloody thing down and have a seat.' He spoke with a voice of absolute authority and Zoe found herself obediently setting the plate down on the broad stone shelf of the mantelpiece then looking around for a place to sit. There were no chairs in the room. Her only options were the bed, which was out of the question, or the low sofa, which wasn't much better.

She elected to perch on the very edge of the sofa. It looked to her like a purpose built seduction couch. And indeed Thor immediately came and sat down beside her, intimately close, exhaling smoke. 'There's a good girl. Now, you're new aren't you?'

'Yes.'

'What's your name?'

'Zoe.' Short answers – monosyllables if possible – seemed the best policy. Zoe judged the distance to the door in case she had to make a run for it. But Thor rose from the sofa and walked away, to one of the high book cases that lined the walls. Zoe began to relax a little again. But her relief was short lived. Thor quickly selected a book and came and sat beside her on the sofa again.

'Look at this,' he said. 'Isn't it fascinating?' The book was a heavy volume bound in red leather with silver decorations set into it. The cover featured a stylised image of what Zoe vaguely recognised as a Celtic knot. 'Can you read?'

'No,' lied Zoe. She felt this was by far the safest policy. But Thor was unperturbed. 'That doesn't matter,' he said, leafing through the book. 'There are plenty of pictures.'

He showed Zoe some of the pictures.

He was leaning close to her, the smell of him, a combination of eau de cologne, tobacco and raw animal musk thick in her nostrils. He caressed the leather cover of the book as he turned the pages for Zoe's supposed delectation. 'This is a very unusual volume,' he murmured. 'Rare and expensive.' He paused at a particularly graphic illustration and held the book open wide to show her. 'A limited edition.'

'Not limited enough,' said Zoe, averting her eyes.

Thor closed the book, set it down beside Zoe, and rose gracefully from the sofa. Zoe hardly dared look up at him. He stood in front of her, wafting the silken hem of his dressing gown as though to allow some unbearable enormous heat to escape. 'You know, you really are a pretty little thing,' he purred. 'I imagine that out of that dreadful maid's outfit, you're a right little cracker.'

'Well, I'm afraid that theory is going to have to remain in the realms of pure speculation,' said Zoe.

Thor roared with laughter. 'You little minx! Fancy talking like that and pretending that you can't read. You're an educated little confection, aren't you?' He kneeled in front of her, forcing Zoe to look him in the eye. His eyes were moss green with a mad sheen to them, as if this were a man who would observe no boundaries. 'I like a bit of education in a woman,' he said. His voice was a deep low rumble. His breath smelled of raw liquor. His mouth moved towards hers.

The door suddenly opened and the Doctor peered in, smiling politely. 'Excuse me for not knocking,' he said. He stepped into the room, giving the mirror over the bureau a curious glance before turning to the couch where Thor was looming over Zoe. 'But I had the feeling that I was needed here.'

'Oh do come in,' murmured Thor, unperturbed. 'Everybody welcome.' He rose to his feet and went to escort the Doctor into the room, closing the door behind him. 'Now I believe you're the Doctor chap, aren't you? One of Pemberton's sawbones pals.'

'I'm not a surgeon, but I am the Doctor.'

'Well excellent, come on in and don't be shy.' He gestured at Zoe, 'I was just getting better acquainted with a new member of staff. Why don't you join me? She's a fascinating little packet.'

'She certainly is,' said the Doctor. 'But I've come here with a different purpose. I want to ask you some questions.'

'Ask away. I'm happy to tell you anything. Anything at all.' Thor took out his cigar and exhaled. 'Nothing quite like a free and frank exchange of ideas.'

The Doctor went and stood beside the sofa, near Zoe. His eyes gleamed as he smiled at Thor. 'What were you doing in the billiard room this morning?'

Thor smiled back. 'Oh, I'm in the billiard room every morning.'

'This the room that your brother believes is exclusively his private domain and into which no one else dares venture?'

Thor chuckled. 'Yes, that would be the one. I'm usually in there quite early. While Roderick is still sluggishly in bed I'm stealing a march on the day, reading the newspapers and enjoying a brandy.'

'So it was your routine to read the newspapers in the room where the body was found. As a way of snubbing your brother.'

'Let us say it has the pleasurable bonus of snubbing him, while allowing me to acquaint myself with the latest world events. And enjoy a decent armagnac.'

'But don't you think it's a little strange to be enjoying a brandy over the dead body of your uncle?'

Thor's smile faded. 'It wasn't exactly over his dead body. I had the armchair turned away at a discreet angle. You're making it sound disgusting.'

'Nevertheless, it seems a trifle odd.' The Doctor turned to Zoe, who nodded in agreement. 'Behaving that way in the room with your uncle's dead body.'

Thor stared at them both with indignation. 'Why, if a man's going to let every little thing interfere with his daily routine . . .'

He strode to the marble dresser, discarded his cigar with a flick of a finger into a deep blue enamel bowl, selected another one, clipped it, lit it, and puffed out a veil of shimmering smoke. 'There would be chaos,' he concluded, taking the cigar from his lips and inspecting it with approval.

'Tell me about the key to the billiard room.'

'What about it?'

'Do you have a copy of it?'

Thor smiled. 'Of course I've got a copy of the key. I imagine every Dutchman, navvy and fiddler's bitch in south east Kent has got one.'

'Your brother doesn't seem to be of the same opinion.'

Thor turned and began to pace the room. 'There are very few areas where Pemberton and I share the same opinion.'

He walked over and sat beside Zoe on the sofa. Without any ceremony or preamble he draped one of his hands on her leg, well above the knee. 'Women, for instance,' he said.

Zoe immediately stood up, dodging away from the warm intrusive hand. She went to the door and turned around. 'I think I'd better be going now,' she said, her voice shaking a little.

Thor was unperturbed. He moved to the Doctor and purred, 'Perhaps you'd help me convince the young lady to experience the further reaches of human pleasure.' He smiled and winked. 'And then, Doctor, you could share in enjoying her obvious charms.' He turned and walked towards Zoe, toying with the long tasselled belt of his silk dressing gown. 'We could open some champagne and make an occasion of it. I haven't had a proper orgy for ages.'

The Doctor smiled politely. 'Who was it who once compared the human sexual impulse to a laboratory rat pressing a button that is wired to its pleasure centres, endlessly pressing and pressing and pressing the button, relentlessly and mechanically, until the rat collapses?'

Thor's face fell. 'Well it certainly wasn't Catullus or Sappho.' He went to the dresser and poured himself a healthy nip from a bottle of brandy. 'You certainly know how to put a damper on things, Doctor.'

'Good,' said the Doctor. 'Now I'd like to ask you a few questions about the murders.'

'Oh so we're calling them murders now, are we? Earlier, they were still being officially described as deaths in the family.'

'Speaking of the family,' said the Doctor, 'Was Colonel Marlowe your uncle by blood or by marriage?'

'By blood of course. He was our father's brother. Why?'

'Because your brother seemed oddly unwilling to answer that simple question.'

'I can't imagine why. Probably just being bloody-minded.'

'Well, thank you for answering my questions.' The Doctor went and joined Zoe by the door.

'You're not going, are you Doctor?' The man suddenly had the vulnerable eyes of a lonely child. 'Surely you have time for a game of chess?' Thor turned to his chessboard with a hungry look.

'No I'm sorry, but we must be going. And I think Zoe would be safer if she came with me.'

'Safer?' Thor chuckled. 'You're depriving me of every possible pleasure, Doctor.' He settled onto his bed and, puffing at his cigar, picked up a newspaper. Zoe got the feeling that they had been dismissed.

But the Doctor was leaving in his own time. 'Be careful Mr Upcott,' he said. Thor looked bleakly at him over the newspaper. 'Why, Doctor?'

'Because I have reason to believe your life is in danger.'

Chapter Eight

The Doctor and Zoe were in the corridor, moving rapidly away from Thor's room when they heard footsteps. They turned to see Pemberton at the far end of the corridor, running towards them. He ran with a strange spavined, splay-footed gait. 'Doctor!' he yelled.

The Doctor and Zoe turned to watch him approach. 'Mr Upcott seems upset about something,' murmured the Doctor. Upcott was running along the corridor at top speed, flailing his long limbs. He careened into a small three legged table with a dusty green potted aspidistra sitting on it and sent the shrub spinning off to crash on the floor, spilling rich black loam on the white marble.

He ran up to them gasping.

'My wife!' he gasped.

Half an hour later Zoe was standing beside the Doctor in the bathroom of the late Mrs Upcott. It was a big room with a fireplace at one end and a view from the north facing window out over the rolling fields of Kent in the direction of Canterbury. A skylight in the sloping roof let in ample daylight on the bathtub, a tall proud creation of cast iron and enamel. In the tub was the dead woman, Millicent Upcott.

She sat there, only her head and shoulders showing in a cooling tub full of soapy water with an incongruous wooden duck floating forlornly on the foamy surface.

Carnacki crouched over her, studying the tattoo on her forehead with a magnifying glass. 'Another red dragon,' he said. The Doctor moved restlessly to the window and peered out at the rolling miles of snow, gleaming in the afternoon sunlight. Zoe joined him.

'So much for your theory about the killer only operating by night, Doctor,' she said in a shaky voice. It helped to try and pretend to be a detective, assisting the Doctor and Carnacki in the investigation of the murder. 'It's still fully daylight.'

The Doctor wagged his head in rapid disagreement. 'I'm not sure I'm quite ready to abandon that theory.' Just then the bathroom door opened and Pemberton Upcott came in, his face drawn and haggard. He looked at them and then went to the bathtub. He crouched beside it, as close as he could get to the body of his wife. He knuckled a tear from his eye.

'Dead,' he said.

The Doctor, Carnacki and Zoe all murmured conventional words of consolation, the way you do when someone is bereaved.

'Murdered,' rasped Pemberton Upcott, his shoulders heaving histrionically.

'Evidently,' said the Doctor.

'Just like the others,' said Pemberton, his voice a raw sob. He closed his eyes and put his face against his wife's cold cheek. 'With not a single incriminating mark left on her body.'

The Doctor and Carnacki exchanged a glance that Pemberton was not meant to see.

Zoe was desperate to ask them what was going on. But this was clearly not the time or place. Pemberton kneeled by the tub, hunched over his wife's body as if protecting her naked form from the gaze of the others in the room, and sobbed quietly.

'Do you remember our encounter with Thor Upcott?'

'I'm hardly likely to forget it,' said Zoe. They were walking down the central staircase of the house with Carnacki, leaving their host to grieve over his dead spouse.

'Well,' continued the Doctor, 'did you notice anything odd about the mirror in his room?' They reached the bottom of the staircase and stood in the main hall of the house.

'The mirror?' said Zoe. 'No. Why?'

Carnacki suddenly interrupted them. 'If you'll excuse me, I want to look in on Celandine.'

'Of course,' said the Doctor, 'In fact we'll accompany you if that's all right.'

'Please.' Carnacki hurried off into the gloom of the west wing. Seeing the dead woman in the tub, and witnessing the grief of her husband, seemed to have shaken him. Zoe and the Doctor followed him to the library where he proceeded to check on Celandine, who was still lying on the low red velvet sofa, still breathing slowly and rhythmically, eyes shut, for all the world like someone peacefully asleep. The Doctor examined her swiftly and looked up at Carnacki. 'You mentioned that she had been talking?'

'The servants look in on her frequently and they've observed the phenomenon. As have I, looking in from time to time. She mutters broken fragments of phrases. Nothing I've been able to make out.'

Carnacki spent the rest of the afternoon sitting with the comatose Celandine. Zoe spent it dodging as many domestic chores as she could. Finally the pale winter sun set and darkness fell. The cold of night began to penetrate the house, invading its bricks as though it were stealing into the bones of a living creature. In the house the servants fought back by stoking the fires in the innumerable fireplaces scattered around Fair Destine.

Under the pretext of attending to the fire in the library, Zoe joined the Doctor and Carnacki, who sat beside Celandine's recumbent form. There was no change in the girl's condition. She looked like she was asleep.

'Tell me,' said the Doctor. 'In Celandine's career as a medium has she ever –' he stopped speaking. There was a loud commotion outside the library door, followed by the unmistakable sound of running feet. 'What the devil's that?' said Carnacki. He followed Zoe and the Doctor to the door. They peered out to see that a terrified mob of guests was hurrying towards the front door, dressed in their winter coats and hats, heavily shod feet thundering on the wooden floor.

'It's like a stampede,' said Zoe.

Carnacki was nonplussed. 'What are they doing?'

'It would appear that they are abandoning the house.' The Doctor stopped the butler, Elder-Main, who was hurrying past, carrying an armful of fur wraps. 'Excuse me,' said the Doctor, 'What's going on?'

'People are very upset about all the murders and so on, sir. Seems everyone's scared that they might be the next victim. So they are all quitting the place, sir. At once. And it's created quite a muddle, I can tell you.'

'What prompted this sudden exodus?'

Elder-Main frowned. 'I believe one of the ladies started to panic sir. And the panic just spread.'

'Like a stampede,' said the Doctor. 'An interesting example of group dynamics in a mammal population.'

'But where do they think they're going?' Carnacki shook his head. 'The blizzard has made the roads impassable.'

'They say they'll strike off overland, sir. It's only ten or twelve miles to Canterbury.'

'In this freezing weather?' said the Doctor. 'Across deep snow drifts? At night?'

'I know, sir,' said Elder-Main, pursing his lips and shaking his head ruefully.

'It's folly,' said the Doctor.

'Especially if they forget to wear their best furs,' said the butler, hurrying away.

Zoe and the others followed him. The entrance hall of the house was like an anthill stirred with a stick. The party guests were surging out of the door into the winter night, some carrying lamps, some with hip flasks and shooting sticks. They were streaming down the steps in a determined fashion, heading for the driveway, garden and dark countryside beyond.

Carnacki and the Doctor stared at the exodus. 'What are we going to do?' said Carnacki. 'We can't just let them rush off to die in the night.' Zoe had a private opinion about that, which she thought was best left unexpressed. They both turned to the Doctor, who seemed about to express an opinion of his own.

Then the screaming started.

The air outside was clean and cold and almost intoxicating in its sweetness, at least to Zoe, who was accustomed to breathing the canned atmosphere of the Space Wheel. She was wearing a borrowed pair of boots that were too tight and pinched and the heavy navy blue overcoat she had stolen when she arrived. Nonetheless she found herself trembling with cold.

The cold didn't seem to bother the Doctor. He had come outside dressed in nothing more substantial than his old jacket. Carnacki had donned some kind of canvas hunting coat trimmed with fur. They had all hurried outside at the sound of the screaming and, with his long legs, Carnacki had been the first to see the cause of it.

He'd taken one look, then hurried off to question the servant. The Doctor and Zoe remained where they were, gazing at it.

About a hundred metres from the house the ground rose up then took a steep dip down towards a small stream that wound across the property. At least, it had once wound across it. Now the snow clad property ended in a sharp rim that excluded the stream and everything beyond it, like a carved piece of cake with white icing.

The edge of the ground had a horrible bitten-off look, as though some unimaginable enormous mouth had chewed away at its perimeter. Beyond that ragged edge of raw loam, there were stars.

'Stars,' whispered Zoe. 'My God, stars.' She stared, her breath rising in tattered luminous whisps on the cold air. She felt light headed, a tremulous sense of vertigo. After all, she had become accustomed to seeing stars in the winter sky, above. But not directly in front of one.

Or *below*.

Zoe stared out at the edge of the garden, where a few hours ago the land had receded gently into the distance, the grounds of Fair Destine giving way to the snow covered fields and hills of Kent. Now there were no fields or hills. Just stars in an infinite black sky that began a hundred metres from the house. Zoe shuddered and hurried to join the Doctor and Carnacki.

They were standing near the bitten-off edge where the snow ended and the sloping dark loam stretched out for a few brief metres before giving way to the star spattered void. 'Look at the stream,' said Carnacki. Zoe saw that the last of the water was draining from the stream, running over the edge of the grounds, off the dark apron of earth and turning into a glittering mist that drifted with great slowness out into the dark void, thinning and dispersing.

'Yes,' said the Doctor. 'It's turning into ice crystals as soon as it hits the vacuum. I wouldn't get too near the edge there, Zoe.'

'You don't need to tell me twice.' She stepped smartly back.

Everyone else was already standing well away from the edge, most of them looking in the opposite direction as though averting their eyes. Staring back towards the house. Not that any of the guests seemed anxious to actually go back inside, to return to the scene of the murders. Instead, they milled about in a dazed confusion, their exodus aborted. Some were openly weeping. Like survivors of a bomb blast, thought Zoe.

But it was a bomb that had gone off in their minds, when they saw what had happened.

'According to the servants it's like this all around the house,' said Carnacki. 'Forming a ragged elliptical perimeter with a circumference of perhaps three hundred yards.'

'And everything else has vanished,' said the Doctor staring up, then down into the night sky. The stars were bright and cold and distant, stark clusters and swirls of them in the dizzyingly deep vaults of infinitely receding space.

'Or we've vanished,' said Carnacki. 'And everything else is still there . . . Somewhere else . . .'

'I don't understand,' said Zoe. She felt like crying.

'About three acres of irregular garden and woodland still surrounds the house,' continued Carnacki calmly. 'Beyond that all is . . . well, as you can see . . . void. Visualised in three dimensions I imagine the house is sitting on what resembles an enormous clod of mud.'

'Which is floating in space.' Zoe followed the Doctor's gaze, looking upwards at the night sky and the sparsely spattered white of the infinite stars. 'Space,' echoed Carnacki. 'The open cosmos. As if we are on the borderland between this world and infinity.'

Zoe looked down from the dark sky and back at the place where the stream had once been, now just a dark winding trench in the snow clad ground, glistening, drained and empty. The stream, the Kentish countryside, England, the rest of the world . . . She stared out at the unlimited dark reaches of the night. Cold constellations without end. She felt her heart sink into her boots. Slowly she backed away, further still from the edge, and then yet further. Still she didn't feel safe. She wondered if she'd ever feel safe again. The endless abyss seemed to threaten to suck her over the side, into the void, to fall forever . . .

'In short,' said the Doctor, 'there is no question of leaving on foot.'

The guests huddled around a fire in the great hall, most of them still wearing their heavy outdoor coats and sweating glumly. Zoe found herself nabbed by Elder-Main and drafted into serving drinks to everyone. She didn't really mind. Everyone looked like they needed a drink.

Except Thor Upcott, who no doubt had had plenty to drink already. He was standing by the east fireplace, braying loudly. 'Well I think it's absolutely extraordinary. I mean it's not every day that the bulk of the family estate ceases to exist and is replaced by the swirling bowels of the cosmos. It almost makes me wish I had a telescope. Well, actually I do. But I mean it makes me wish I knew something about astronomy. I'd take a crack at looking at all those constellations and milky ways and things.'

Zoe wished he would shut up. But it seemed there was no one who was both inclined and qualified to tell him to do so. The older brother, Pemberton, who might normally be expected to provide this service, was sitting on a sofa staring into some confused inner space. No one sat too near to him, allowing him the traditional respectful isolation of the recently bereaved. Zoe thought of the poor woman upstairs in the bath. The water slowly forming a film of ice around her as the chill of winter invaded the room.

As soon as she had finished serving drinks – warm pewter mugs of mulled rum with spiced butter floating on it – Zoe took the tray back to the kitchen and then hurried upstairs to join the Doctor and Carnacki. They were once again busy in Mrs Upcott's bathroom.

'How is everyone downstairs?' said the Doctor.

'Pretty downcast,' said Zoe. 'Either waiting for the killer to strike again or still trying to come to grips with the new boundaries of the estate.'

'Oh I don't think they need to worry about the killer. At least not most of them . . . ' said the Doctor. He was standing beside Carnacki, bending down over the tub. The terribly still white form of Mrs Upcott was sitting in the opaque white water with ice crystals slowly forming at the base of her neck. Her long smooth white arms were extended out over either side of the tub.

'Only Thor Upcott seems the least bit cheerful,' said Zoe.

'Yes. Our friend Thor. He is an exception in many ways. Not least an exception to my observation about the killer. Thor, I believe, does indeed have something to fear.' The Doctor turned to Carnacki. 'Can I borrow your magnifying glass?' Carnacki passed it to him. The Doctor peered at the woman's forehead where a tiny red dragon marred the pale skin, like a fresh wound.

'Is her tattoo just like the others?' said Zoe. She found herself speaking in a whisper, as if she were afraid the dead woman might hear her. 'Not quite like the others,' said the Doctor, handing the magnifying glass back to Carnacki.

He offered it to Zoe and she quickly shook her head. 'I'll leave that to you.' Carnacki once again inspected the tattoo with his magnifying glass. Then he took out a small bottle of clear liquid and a white rag. Zoe turned to the Doctor. 'I'm very sorry about what has happened to Mrs Upcott and the others.' She glanced at the bath where Carnacki was busy, dampening the rag with liquid from the jar. He bent over and dabbed the rag on the dead woman's forehead. Zoe looked away, turning back to the Doctor. 'But instead of devoting all our time to looking for the killer, shouldn't we also be looking for Jamie? He might be in terrible danger.'

'We might all be,' said the Doctor matter of factly. 'But in the meantime look at this.' He nodded to Carnacki who showed her the white rag. There was a tiny red smudge on it.

'What is it? Blood?'

Carnacki shook his head. 'As far as we can tell it's some kind of indelible ink.'

'Not entirely indelible, though.' Carnacki showed her the small bottle. 'White spirits. Methyl alcohol. We managed to remove some with this.'

'So now we know what is causing the tattoos. Someone is drawing them on with this ink.'

'No. That's the odd thing,' said the Doctor. He turned to look at Mrs Upcott, sitting in her cold bath. 'It's only this one that shows any evidence of being drawn on with ink. The others actually appear to be pigmentation in the skin cells. Tattooed or something very like it.'

'So why is this one different?' said Zoe.

'Come and look at this,' said Carnacki. Zoe swallowed and joined him by the bathtub. Carnacki took the woman's right arm and gently moved it so Zoe could see the skin, delicate and flawless and pale as ivory with the faintest hint of blue indicating where a vein had once flowed. By lowering her wrist, Carnacki exposed the flesh on the inside of the elbow. 'Do you see that?' He offered Zoe the magnifying glass and this time she took it.

'See what?'

'There. Look.' Zoe saw it. The glass revealed a tiny blush of purple bruising, so faint as to be almost undetectable, and just the suggestion of an indentation. Zoe lowered the magnifying glass. 'What is it?'

'The mark of a needle,' said the Doctor. 'A rather large hypodermic needle.' He looked at the dead woman. 'Which accounts for the lethal sleep of the unfortunate Mrs Upcott.'

'Are you familiar with morphine?' said Carnacki to Zoe. 'It is one of the alkaloids of opium, and it is enormously potent.'

'You mean Mrs Upcott was an addict and she overdosed?'

The Doctor shook his head. 'There's no evidence of any other needle marks. We think someone else deliberately injected her and killed her.'

'And we think we know who,' said Carnacki.

'Who?' said Zoe.

'None other than her husband the distinguished surgeon, Pemberton Upcott, using a syringe from his medical bag and morphine from his pharmacoepia.'

Zoe looked at the dead woman in the tub and felt an odd rush of relief. 'So there was nothing supernatural involved after all.'

'Nothing supernatural?' snorted Carnacki. He pointed out the window at the infinite glowing void that now began where the garden ended. 'Oh yes,' said Zoe. 'That.'

Chapter Nine

The wine cellar of Fair Destine was reached by passing through a heavy oak door in the rear of the pantry and descending a long stone staircase. 'I understand there is a series of cellars under the house,' said the Doctor. 'Yes sir,' said Elder-Main. 'Even got one full of nothing but fireworks, for the celebration of special occasions. But this one, where we keep the wine, is walled off from the others with no access except up the stairs and through that one door, which as you see is fixed with a very heavy lock operated by that key you saw.'

'To keep the help out of the wine,' added Thor Upcott drily.

There were no windows in the wine cellar, just some narrow slits for ventilation, set high in the walls close to the ceiling. The place was predictably cold and shockingly damp. 'Just as well you're wearing your long johns,' said Thor.

His brother frowned at him and said nothing. Zoe had no idea if Pemberton really was wearing long johns, but he had sensibly wrapped himself up in several sweaters and scarves under a large fur coat. He turned to the Doctor and Carnacki and said, 'When I get out of here there is going to be hell to pay.'

The Doctor smiled sweetly and said, 'I'm sorry if you're uncomfortable here but it's only a temporary measure. As soon as everything's all right again the police will be called in.'

'And until that time I am to be locked in my own wine cellar,' said Pemberton bitterly.

'*Our* wine cellar, old man,' corrected Thor.

His brother stared at him with hatred. 'That's right, isn't it? You will never let me forget that half the estate is yours, whereas you want all of it. And it's the only reason you're going along with this charade.'

Thor Upcott murmured, 'On the contrary, I'm inclined to believe the Doctor and Mr Carnacki.' Pemberton turned his furious gaze on the Doctor and Carnacki. 'How can you?' he demanded of Thor. 'They're suggesting that I murdered my own wife.'

'Well, you did have the means, opportunity and motive, old son,' drawled Thor. 'Particularly the motive. I know how little love was lost between you and Millicent.'

'Mendacious claptrap! I did love her.'

'Perhaps once, a long time ago, before the hen began to peck, eh?'

'You know nothing about me, or my marriage. I loved my wife. I could never harm her. How can you accuse me of murder? I'm innocent.' He looked at Thor. 'And you know it. You just want the entire estate for your own.'

Thor chuckled. 'It may have escaped your notice, dear brother, but the bulk of estate has vanished. In fact we are floating in the naked void.'

Carnacki cleared his throat. 'Which reminds me. I must resume my enquiries into the exact nature of our disappearance and our current strange situation.'

'And see if there isn't a way to restore things to the way they were,' added the Doctor. With these words he and Carnacki turned towards the steps that led up out of the wine cellar. Zoe hurried to join them. She'd had enough of the cold and damp; and of Pemberton. Thor followed her, a little too close for comfort.

'So you're just going to leave me here!' shouted Pemberton. They glanced back at him. He was standing watching them like a cornered animal. But Zoe couldn't work up much sympathy for the man. The wine cellar was as cold and grim as any dungeon, but Pemberton had been provided with plenty of blankets and cushions, an anodised bucket with a wooden lid for sanitary purposes, a lamp and books, and a picnic basket full of delectables.

'And he certainly won't be short of a bottle of wine or two,' said Thor, locking the door behind them and dropping the key in his pocket. 'In fact it's probably worth snuffing the spouse for the opportunity to be locked up with all the old Chateau Margaux!' He barked a laugh and strutted off through the pantry and out of the kitchen.

The Doctor joined Carnacki in the west dining room where he was setting up what he described as his 'apparatus', which to Zoe looked like a random jumble of very primitive electrical equipment. The Doctor, however, was fascinated and eager to get involved and assist Carnacki in his preparations. Zoe watched in growing frustration. 'How is any of this going to help us find Jamie?' she demanded.

The Doctor paused from braiding a wire and smiled at her and said, 'I don't know exactly, but I expect it will, somehow, in the end.' Zoe sighed and left. Even her domestic servant duties were more interesting than this and she willingly spent a few hours working in the kitchen and the ground floor of the house, distributing refreshments to the guests.

The entire atmosphere in the house had changed since the announcement of Pemberton's house arrest in the wine cellar. Along with all the predictable shock and disbelief that their host could be a murderer, there had come a profound wave of relief. The killer in their midst had at last been identified and neutralised. Zoe shared in the relief. No one seemed too concerned about the fact that their shared horizon terminated abruptly a few hundred metres from the house and that they were existing on a tiny clump of earth surrounded by a minuscule air bubble floating in the dizzying, endless immensity of the void.

The general consensus seemed to be that now the killer was under lock and key, everything would sort itself out.

As the long day, as measured by the slow ticking of the grandfather clock in the hallway, drew to a close, Zoe found herself yawning. She had been awake for what seemed an eternity. Soon her duties would be at an end, the night staff would take over and she could retire to her hard, narrow bed in the servants' quarters.

She was sitting in front of the coal fire in the servant's refectory, taking off her shoes and massaging her feet, when Elder-Main came in and handed her an envelope. 'For you,' he said unhelpfully, and hurried out. The envelope was made of a heavy creamy paper with ridges embossed on it. In the centre of the envelope, in black ink and copperplate script, was written *Zoe*.

Zoe hesitated, then ripped the envelope open with her finger. Inside was a brief note, written on the same heavy cream paper as the envelope, in the same handwriting. Folded in with it was what Zoe at first took to be some kind of document or certificate. It was only after a second and third inspection of the large, official-looking piece of paper that she realised that it was in fact money. A five pound note.

The note read: *No, please don't thank me my dear. I have not been too generous. You are no doubt worth every penny. Kindly join me in my room at midnight for an unforgettable interlude.*

It was signed *Thor*, and there was a PS: *Please bring an assortment of sandwiches, some cold meats and cheese and a small soufflé if you think you can whip up a decent one.*

The five pound note burned with an agreeable fierce glow when chucked into the fire, followed shortly by the note and the envelope. Zoe slept like a log that night on the narrow slab of her maid's bed and woke up the following morning refreshed and ready to face another day. Although of course the concept of morning and day were hard to grasp for most of the other people in the house, since they were floating in the perpetual night of deep space.

Zoe bathed as well as she could in the primitive conditions on offer, dressed in her uniform, and went off to find the Doctor. She found him still busy in the west wing dining room where Carnacki's electrical contraption had begun to take shape. A large ring of glass was erected vertically on the big dinner table, like a hoop waiting for a circus animal to jump through it. It was about a metre in diameter and consisted of a thin curved tube of milky glass of slightly greater than finger thickness.

The hoop was held in place by twin bronze armatures, which rested on felt padded discs of bronze. On either side of the hoop were heavy mahogany boxes that contained some kind of batteries. Two more mahogany boxes full of bulbous glowing vacuum tubes were connected to these on either side by thick spools of silver wire.

The Doctor was standing on the table, with a pair of wire cutters in his teeth, making some final adjustments to the vacuum tubes. He glanced up as Zoe came in. Carnacki was sitting nearby, staring pensively out of the window at the dark sky and the intricate swirl of stars.

'What is it?' said Zoe, immediately sensing the mood in the room.

The Doctor hopped down off the table and took the wire cutters out of his mouth. 'It's Thor Upcott.'

'What about him?' demanded Zoe, reddening as she recalled the assignation she had refused last night. But even before Carnacki rose from his chair and came over, his face grim, she knew the answer.

'He was killed last night.' Carnacki sounded exhausted. 'In the same manner as the others. No mark on the body but a red dragon tattooed on the forehead.'

'But Pemberton is locked away in the wine cellar.'

'Oh we never really suspected Pemberton of being the killer,' said the Doctor.

'Then why did you lock him up?'

'The Doctor means we never suspected him of being *the* killer,' said Carnacki. 'If that makes sense.'

'No it doesn't,' said Zoe, who felt an urge to scream. The Doctor smiled patiently and tried to explain. 'Some mysterious force or agency is committing a series of murders in this house, leaving a distinctive hallmark each time. Yes?'

'Yes,' repeated Zoe wearily.

'Good. But we don't suspect Pemberton of being responsible for these. Instead we think that he killed his wife, whose murder does not match the pattern of the others.'

Zoe realised Carnacki was holding something up for her to see. It was a small wooden box lined with black velvet. Inside it, in form fitted compartments, lay a large glass and chrome syringe. In a glass drawer at one end of the box were a selection of needles. 'From Pemberton Upcott's study.' Carnacki set it down and picked up a small bottle with a yellow label. Written on it in slanting green ink was MORPHINE – POISON. 'We believe these are the murder weapons.'

'But only as far as his wife is concerned?' said Zoe.

'Correct. None of the other bodies shows needle marks. And crucially, none of them shows any signs of the red dragon being drawn on with ink. Instead they are tattoos.'

'We expect some red ink and a pen to turn up in Pemberton's effects soon,' said the Doctor. 'Who would have thought he was such an accomplished artist?'

'Needs must,' said Carnacki, 'when the devil drives.'

Elder-Main appeared in the doorway. The butler seemed haggard and beaten down. He stared distractedly at Zoe, Carnacki and the Doctor, as though trying to remember what had brought him to them.

'It's Mr Pemberton,' he said finally. 'He wants to see Mr Carnacki and the Doctor, pronto.'

The wine cellar was, if anything, more cold and uninviting than on their previous visit. Pemberton Upcott was sitting on his lidded bucket, wrapped in a blanket, glowering at them.

'All right, look here. I'm willing to lay my cards on the table providing I receive certain concessions.'

'I told them, sir,' said Elder-Main. Pemberton ignored him. 'In short I want to be let out of this freezing filthy cellar and back upstairs like a civilised man.'

'A civilised man who is also a murderer,' said Carnacki. Pemberton glared at him then looked at the floor. 'That's what I mean by laying my cards on the table. I'm willing to admit to doing that. I killed my wife, but I categorically deny the other murders.'

He caught Zoe's eye. He seemed to want to explain to her. 'I won't be a menace to anyone. It was only her I hated. I couldn't pass up the opportunity.' Zoe turned away from him. 'Opportunity?' she said. 'What does he mean?'

'I mean the God-sent opportunity to conceal my own crime. These other murders were the perfect alibi. I could kill her and no one would be any the wiser.'

'Why do that?' Zoe turned and confronted Pemberton. 'Why not just wait until the killer did the job for you?'

'Because whoever is doing the killing is pursuing my family blood line, as the Doctor was all too quick to spot. I had every reason to think that my wife would be spared. So I had to dispense with her myself.' He stood up, moving painfully slowly, his knee joints clicking. 'Now can I go upstairs and sit beside a fire?'

Zoe turned to the Doctor. 'If it's not him, who is the killer?'

'Who or what?' said the Doctor. 'I suspect the answer will reveal itself as we set about the business of taking this house back to reality as we know it. And I somehow suspect that it's all tied in with whatever has happened to Jamie.'

He turned towards the staircase. 'But first we have another murder scene to visit.'

Chapter Ten

Thor Upcott had ended his life as Zoe imagined he had lived a large portion of it, reclining on his seduction couch, in his silk dressing gown, with his hand clasped to his groin.

In the centre of the dead man's forehead was the trademark red dragon. Carnacki set aside the bottle of white spirit and the rag. He glanced at the Doctor. 'No trace of ink. Authentic tattoo this time.'

'As we suspected,' said the Doctor. He turned away from the body and walked the length of the bedroom. From the doorway Elder-Main watched nervously. The Doctor paused as he walked past the marble topped bureau that held the now reliquary debris of Thor Upcott's cosmetic vanity, and his enthusiastic dipsomania. The Doctor turned abruptly to this bureau and swept aside the bottles of cologne and cognac.

Elder-Main ran forward into the room and stopped in shock near the Doctor. 'Don't break anything sir – ' he said. The Doctor seemed to not hear him. He was staring across the now cleared space of the bureau at the mirror mounted on the wall above. 'Zoe, do you remember me saying to you that there was something odd about this mirror?'

Zoe came over and joined him, glad to leave Thor Upcott's corpse to Carnacki's attentions. 'Yes, I remember you mentioning something.'

The Doctor was staring at the mirror. 'What do you notice about it?' Elder-Main was watching the Doctor, visibly trembling with anxiety as he hastily rearranged the bottles on the bureau. He seemed afraid that the Doctor was about to smash something delicate and priceless, ruining it forever. Zoe studied the mirror. 'For one thing,' she said, 'It's positioned so that someone on the couch – the seduction couch – can see themselves reflected in it.'

'Alternatively,' said the Doctor, staring into the strange gaze of his own reflection, 'it is so positioned as to provide a good view of the couch for someone standing behind the mirror.'

'Behind the mirror?'

Elder-Main suddenly gave a little tremor and a moan and said, 'All right, sir. You don't need to keep on with the cat and mouse game.'

The Doctor turned to him in astonishment. 'What do you mean?'

'I confess,' said the butler. Everyone stared at him. 'What on earth are you talking about, man?' demanded Carnacki, rising from Thor's body. 'Are you saying that you committed these murders?'

The butler, thought Zoe. The butler did it. No, it couldn't be.

In fact, Elder-Main was shaking his head vigorously. 'Not the murders sir, no. This is what I'm talking about.' He went to the bookshelf to the right of the dresser and pulled out a volume by de Sade. There was an immediate metallic click and the matching bookshelf on the other side of the dresser swung out from the wall, hinging like a door. 'All I'm confessing to is being inside there . . . And watching.'

Elder-Main pulled the bookcase door fully open revealing a space behind, which he entered in what was obviously a familiar routine. The others followed him into a shallow cavity inside the wall, like a half-width corridor. This narrow space, its walls lined with rough lathes, extended either way into shadowy cobwebbed darkness, perhaps winding throughout the entire house. The space was dark except for immediately beside them, where a wide band of light entered via the mirror in Thor Upcott's bedroom. From this side of the wall it was as transparent as window glass, though with an odd silvery sheen to it. 'A two way mirror,' said the Doctor. 'Much as I surmised.'

'I don't understand,' said Carnacki.

'Mr Thor liked to have someone in here in the viewing gallery, sir,' explained Elder-Main. 'To watch him when he was . . . entertaining. He said it gingered him up.'

'I see,' said Carnacki, although he still sounded baffled. 'And how long has this arrangement obtained?'

'Oh, years and years, sir. Ever since Mr Thor had the mirror installed.'

'I see,' repeated Carnacki, his voice growing tight with excitement as he began to see the implications. The Doctor watched in silence, letting Carnacki take the lead. 'And you were in here last night . . .' The butler looked at him in the dim light from the mirror and suddenly turned and hurried back into the bedroom. The others followed him. Elder-Main closed the bookcase behind them, sealing off the passage. Then he turned and stared at them with a haunted look.

'Mr Carnacki's right,' said the Doctor. 'You were in there last night and you saw the murder take place.'

Elder-Main went to the bureau and pulled the stopper out of a crystal decanter with shaking hands. He poured himself a large glass of whisky, slopped some soda into it, and swallowed the concoction in a single gulp. Then he closed his eyes for a moment, his colour deepening, opened them again and spoke in an oddly calm voice.

'I did indeed sir, but you won't like it.'

'What do you mean?' demanded Carnacki.

Elder-Main nodded at Zoe. 'It was her was supposed to come and visit Mr Thor last night. He gave her a fiver as well, misplaced generosity if you ask me. But he always had a generous nature, Mr Thor. Then he put on his best toilet water and favourite dressing gown and lay down on the sofa to wait there for her while I was stationed in the viewing gallery, behind the mirror. I was supposed to watch them.' He looked at Zoe with disapproval. 'But she didn't turn up. Someone else did.'

'Who for God's sake?'

The butler looked bleakly at Carnacki. 'Your friend sir. Miss Celandine Gibson, the celebrated medium.'

'The man is obviously unreliable,' said Carnacki. 'His breath was reeking with whisky. Did you notice?' He glanced at Zoe and the Doctor, who stood by the window of the west dining room. Like all the other windows in Fair Destine, these looked out onto a darkness more profound than any night.

'Yes, he reeked of whisky,' said the Doctor. 'But only after he broke down and confessed.'

Carnacki was busy with his contraption, connecting the batteries in their big mahogany boxes up to the wide delicate glass hoop he'd mounted on the table. Now he looked up at the Doctor angrily. 'What are you saying? That you give credence to his ridiculous story?' He turned to catch Zoe's eyes but she looked away, not wishing to meet his gaze. Instead she peered at the constellations outside the window and realised with a deep cold thrill that they were different from the ones you'd expect to see from the Earth, in 1900. Or any other year.

The Doctor was unperturbed by Carnacki's anger. 'What I'm saying is that the man was stone cold sober when he confessed what he saw and that I believe he was in full command of his wits.'

'Exactly,' said Carnacki, tightening a brass screw to hold down a braid of silver wire. 'He was cold and calculating, a shrewd liar.'

'You're contradicting yourself,' said the Doctor.

'No I'm not. The man was clearly a liar. You surely didn't believe his story? Celandine, entering Thor Upcott's bedroom, moving like a sleepwalker? Bending over the disconcerted but amenable Thor and . . .' Carnacki faltered. 'And then the most ridiculous part. Her kissing him.' He looked up suddenly and caught Zoe's gaze before she could look away. 'He said it was her kiss that killed.' He stood up abruptly and shoved the big battery roughly into place. 'The kiss of death, delivered by Celandine Gibson.' He was trying to sound flippant but again his voice faltered. He turned away from Zoe and flipped a switch on the side of the battery. He moved around the table to the battery on the other side. 'Anyway, I looked in on Celandine, immediately after he told his ridiculous story.'

'We know,' said Zoe gently. 'We were there.'

Carnacki looked at her again, his eyes blank with distraction and torment. He had been profoundly shocked by the butler's revelations and had rushed to Celandine's side. She had been lying on the sofa in the library, eyes closed, breathing softly. 'She was asleep,' said Carnacki. 'Just like she has been ever since that night. Innocently asleep.'

'But she is a medium,' said the Doctor in his most reasonable and persuasive voice. 'She is naturally open to outside influences . . .'

'Celandine is not a murderess!'

'If she was under the influence of some outer force, then it wasn't

Celandine acting that way.'

'Sophistry,' snarled Carnacki. 'I repeat to you, Celandine Gibson is not responsible. She is not the guilty party. She is not a killer.'

'You have an alternative theory?' said the Doctor pleasantly.

'The ghost of Roderick Upcott is the culprit. When the dead can't rest, they rise and prey on the living. The dead, do you hear? Not Celandine.' He viciously twisted a silver wire onto the second battery. 'These killings are the work of Roderick Upcott, risen from the grave. And I intend to prove it.'

He threw the switch on the second battery and the glass hoop began to glow with a pure streaming white brightness that briefly filled the room. But then the hoop began to dim and silently sputtered out.

Carnacki frowned. 'Damn. It's still malfunctioning. It's as if it's getting interference from something.'

'Such as?' said the Doctor.

Carnacki was calming down now, becoming caught up in the abstractions of the technical problem. 'I don't know. Some powerful object nearby.'

'And what might that be, I wonder,' said the Doctor. He glanced at a large leather case lying on the sideboard opposite the table. Zoe recognised it as the case containing the Spirit Lance of Cornwall, the subject of Carnacki's lecture.

'Of course!' cried Carnacki, rushing to the sideboard. 'It's the lance interfering with my device. You're a genius, Doctor.' He hefted the case containing the lance and lugged it out of the door. While he was gone the Doctor winked at Zoe and swiftly altered one of the electrical connections on Carnacki's device. Then he stood away from it, just before Carnacki returned. Carnacki no longer had the lance. 'I put it down the far end of the corridor. That should do the trick.'

He returned to his apparatus on the table, made some final adjustments, and threw the switches. This time the hoop lit up with a steady milky glow. The enormous brightness they'd observed a moment earlier returned slowly. Flickering strands of brightness like silent miniature lightning bolts danced inside the perimeter of the glass hoop. Zoe watched in fascination.

'What's happening, Doctor?'

The Doctor smiled. 'Ask Carnacki. He created this fascinating device.'

'It's quite simple,' said Carnacki. 'The glass ring is tuned to an etheric vibration so as to pick up any local disturbance on the supernatural plane. In the presence of some sort of entity from another dimension, the ring gathers a brilliant pure light at its centre. As you can see is happening here.'

'And what's the point of it?' said Zoe, cutting short the technical explanation.

'Once the light reaches a certain critical strength it flows off in the direction of the etheric disturbance, indicating the origin, or the cause of it.'

As he spoke, the miniature bolts of lightning dancing inside the hoop surged together, coalescing into a disc of pure white. The disc expanded to fill the hoop and suddenly poured forth from it, like the beam from a searchlight.

The hoop wrenched around violently on its twin armatures and Carnacki hastened to shift the apparatus. 'It's seeking its true direction! The glass hoop mustn't break.' The Doctor swiftly assisted Carnacki. 'Thank you,' muttered the man. 'I must design some kind of universal gimbal to hold it, something that will swivel in any direction.'

The glass hoop was now pointing squarely at one of the dining room windows, pouring its light out into the snow swathed grounds and the endless night. 'Look Doctor,' said Zoe.

The light blazed out into the garden and illuminated in sharp relief the gaunt outlines of the spirit gate. 'Of course,' said the Doctor. He turned towards the door, moving quickly but not as quickly as Carnacki, who was already running out of the room and towards the staircase.

Zoe hurried after the Doctor. 'I don't know what all the fuss is about,' she said. 'I told you to look at the spirit gate days ago.'

'It would seem the time was not yet ripe,' said the Doctor. 'But now events are gathering speed.'

'I wish they'd slow down a bit,' said Zoe as they reached the bottom of the stairs and the main entrance hall where Carnacki was throwing on his canvas overcoat. He drew something out of his pocket and Zoe saw the dull glint of a pistol and winced. She hated it when they started taking out guns.

'I suggest that we prepare ourselves for anything, Doctor. This spirit gate could be the portal through which monstrosities from another plane gain access to ours. Who knows what beastly shape this killer really has.'

He was turning to open the front door when Elder-Main appeared. 'She's gone walking again, sir,' he said quietly. Carnacki froze, then turned slowly around. 'What do you mean?'

'Miss Gibson, sir,' said the butler. 'She's up and on the prowl again.'

'Nonsense!' Carnacki turned and ran to the library, the Doctor and Zoe following. He flung the door open and they all stepped in to find the low sofa bed empty. 'She's gone.'

'She was moving like a sleepwalker,' said Elder-Main, drifting through the doorway behind them.

'It's you!' cried Carnacki. 'You've done something with her.' He threw himself towards Elder-Main, but the Doctor restrained him.

'This is madness,' Carnacki shook himself free and turned his back on the butler. 'Celandine is not the killer. I still believe Roderick Upcott lives. Who knows what effect it had on his cadaver, being blasted out of his last resting place by a million volts of electricity?'

'No, it's your lady, sir,' insisted the butler doggedly. 'Walking in her sleep and heading towards the arboretum.'

'The arboretum, you say?' Carnacki flung himself through the door and his footsteps could be heard outside the library, racing in that direction. Zoe moved to follow, but the Doctor hung back for a moment, speaking to the butler in a confidential tone.

'The other day you mentioned fireworks . . . ?'

'Certainly. Half a ton, sir, in the cellar next to the wine cellar.'

'Would you be good enough to get them out,' said the Doctor.

'All of them sir?'

'All of them. And pile them around the spirit gate. I think we might be in for a pyrotechnical display before the night's out.'

Chapter Eleven

The revolving door of the arboretum swished as they pushed through it into the warm perfumed air. Zoe followed the Doctor into the tall structure, thick with lush greenery and heavy with the moist smell of loam and growing things. Carnacki was waiting for them. His eyes were glowing with excitement and he looked very young. 'I've found someone,' he said.

'Celandine?'

'No, someone else. Come and look.' He led them to the far side of the arboretum, past a small verdigrised fountain that bubbled over a sloping bed of plantings, through dense ferns and past beautiful nutating orchids with delicate blue and white markings resembling fine china. They finally came to a corner shrouded by elephant plants with great hanging green leaves. Passing through these they found themselves in a secluded bower where nothing grew but dense clusters of red and white poppies.

And lying there among the countless small blank alert petalled faces lay a young man. 'Jamie!' Zoe leapt forward, crushing poppies under foot. The Doctor followed, picking his way more delicately. It was Jamie all right. Zoe cradled his head in her lap. 'Doctor, what's wrong with him?'

'He's in some kind of trance,' said Carnacki.

'Like Celandine?' Zoe stroked Jamie's forehead. His skin felt dry and warm.

'No,' said Carnacki staring at the unmoving body. 'Deeper. More profound.'

The Doctor examined Jamie swiftly and expertly. 'Indeed. Perhaps a laudanum-induced trance.'

'Laudanum?'

'Yes.' the Doctor gestured impatiently around them. 'Look where he is lying. All around him . . . opium poppies.' Zoe looked at the flowers, their lush scent seemed suddenly to fill the hot house.

'Why poppies?'

The Doctor frowned. 'Someone – or something – is taking revenge on the Upcotts for the devastating suffering they caused by their involvement in the opium trade in the eighteenth and nineteenth centuries, when they helped turn the Chinese into a nation of addicts. This family was knee deep in that whole despicable historical episode.'

'How do you know?' said Zoe.

'I found a ledger in the library that makes the extent of their responsibility all too clear. It contains lavish details of Roderick Upcott's buccaneering days in China.'

'Doctor, look,' interrupted Carnacki in a low, awed voice. The Doctor and Zoe followed the direction of his gaze. All Zoe could see were poppies, lush red and white blossoms, filling the bower and her field of vision. 'What is it?'

'The poppies,' said the Doctor. 'They're growing.'

'What do you mean, growing?' said Zoe. But even as she spoke she saw new blossoms springing into view, rising from the rich loam, sprouting petals. All around her new poppies were bursting out in bright clumps of colour. At first Zoe blinked, unable to believe it, but there was nothing wrong with her eyes. The poppies were soon a thick moist carpet of red with milky splashes of white. She could feel them crowding around her ankles, pressing against her calves. The soft rustling sound of their growth gradually made itself heard in the awe-struck silence.

'Extraordinary,' said the Doctor. 'I wonder what's causing it.' He darted out of the bower then swiftly returned. 'Whatever's responsible for the accelerated growth is only operating on the poppies. None of the other plants seem to be affected.'

Zoe hitched Jamie's body further up against her own. His unmoving form was threatening to vanish under the swelling carpet of vegetation. 'We should get him out of here.'

Carnacki plunged his hands down into the swelling mass of flowers and picked one. 'This is magic,' he said, examining the flower's blind red face. 'Magic pure and simple.'

'Ancient Chinese sorcery perhaps,' said the Doctor.

Carnacki put the poppy in his buttonhole. 'What makes you say that?'

The Doctor looked at Zoe. 'Remember Canton, a hundred years ago? Perhaps the Imperial Astrologer knew what he was doing after all.'

Carnacki leaned in close to them. 'Are you saying you might know who is responsible for this extraordinary display Doctor?'

'Possibly.'

'And do you think this Imperial Astrologer chap might also be capable of conjuring up a demon? A supernatural assassin of some kind?'

'I wouldn't rule it out.'

'Then we have our answer,' said Carnacki. 'This Chinese astrologer has caused Roderick Upcott to awaken from the dead and slay his own descendants.'

'I don't think it can be as simple as that,' said the Doctor.

'Simple?' said Zoe. But she was too distracted to be properly annoyed at this ridiculous remark. Ever since Carnacki had uttered the words 'supernatural assassin' she'd thought she could hear the sound of soft footsteps approaching.

The Doctor looked up alertly. 'What's that?' he said, and Zoe realised that she was indeed hearing footsteps. Carnacki was still wearing his coat. Now he dug hastily in the pocket and pulled out his revolver. 'Someone's coming,' he murmured. The Doctor looked at the gun and said, 'I'm not sure that's such a good idea. You won't be able to use it on Celandine, will you?'

'Damn you, Doctor,' said Carnacki, 'How many times must I repeat myself? It isn't Celandine.'

As it transpired, he was right. A figure paused at the entrance to the bower, ducked and entered. It was Elder-Main. He stared at the profusion of poppies in bewilderment. 'Lord. The cold air certainly hasn't affected these little beauties.' He looked at the Doctor. 'Mr Pemberton was afraid the draughts were going to play havoc with the growth, you know.'

Carnacki pocketed his revolver in exasperation. 'What are you doing here?' The Doctor replied on behalf of the butler. 'I asked him to report to me as soon as certain preparations were complete.' He looked at Elder-Main, his eyes glittering. 'Is everything ready?'

'Yes, sir. I've arranged the fireworks just like you said. And sprinkled around plenty of black powder and left the other barrels under the fireworks. If the whole lot was to go up at once there wouldn't be much left of that old spirit gate.'

'That's very much my idea,' said the Doctor, grinning toothily.

'Spirit gate?' said Carnacki. 'What are you up to Doctor?'

'I should imagine what I'm up to is pretty clear.' The Doctor smiled.

'You intend to blow it up?'

'I intend to blow it out of existence, with a little luck.'

'Are you sure that's advisable?'

The Doctor smiled wolfishly. 'We may not have a full explanation for the strange events which have taken place here.' He gestured towards the glass walls of the arboretum, and beyond them the infinite black skies of space, studded with alien constellations. 'But one thing is certain. There must be a source of energy that has powered them.'

'And that's the spirit gate?' said Zoe.

'It is a dimensional portal allowing the transfer of matter. Why not energy?'

'I'm sure you're the expert in these matters,' conceded Carnacki with a worried frown. 'But are you sure we should just dynamite the thing?'

'Not dynamite sir, black powder,' said Elder-Main.

Carnacki kept his eyes fixed on the Doctor. 'You are hoping that when the spirit gate is destroyed this chunk of land, bearing Fair Destine and the grounds and all of us will be restored to the Earth, to England, to Kent, where it came from?'

'Indeed,' said the Doctor succinctly.

'But what if it doesn't?' persisted Carnacki. Zoe shared his reservations. What if, for instance, destroying the gate merely caused their tiny bubble of atmosphere to blow away, leaving the house hanging in raw screaming vacuum? She shuddered.

'Come along now,' chided the Doctor. 'Where's your sense of adventure?'

Elder-Main suddenly gave a start. 'Who's that?' he said, looking at Jamie.

'I only just noticed him there. He's almost buried under those poppies. He's not . . .'

'Dead? No,' said the Doctor. 'The young gentleman is a companion of mine who went missing when he first arrived here.'

Elder-Main shook his head disapprovingly. 'He shouldn't be asleep in the arboretum like that. What's the matter? Has he had a skinful?'

'We have no idea. But I suspect something more sinister is behind his deep slumber.' The Doctor stepped out of the bower and the others followed, Zoe reluctantly. 'Doctor, we can't just leave him there like that.'

'I have no intention of doing so,' said the Doctor, striding towards the revolving door that led back into the house. 'We are going to collect a variety of smelling salts and other stimulants from Pemberton Upcott's well equipped medical chest and see if we can't wake Jamie.'

'But we've already tried all those on Celandine,' said Carnacki, 'to no avail.'

'But as you yourself pointed out, Jamie's condition appears quite different from Celandine's. Perhaps what didn't work for her will work perfectly well for him.'

'Perhaps,' said Carnacki sceptically. They had now reached the revolving door and paused outside it. 'I'll go,' said Elder-Main. 'I'll fetch the smelling salts and so on. They're all laid out in the library ready. It won't take a moment and you can stay here and keep an eye on your young friend in the poppy bower.'

'Excellent idea,' said the Doctor, 'Except in one particular. Send someone else back with those items. I want you to go outside and prepare to ignite the fireworks on my signal.'

'Your signal?' The Doctor took out a large silver whistle on a chain. 'Is that a policeman's whistle?' said Carnacki. The Doctor nodded and blew gently into the whistle, causing all of them to cover their ears.

'I get the picture, sir,' said Elder-Main 'When you blow it, I'll do it.'

'Yes and not until then. Is that clear? At my signal, light the fuse to detonate the entire pile of pyrotechnical splendour.' The Doctor smiled grimly. 'And be sure to retire to a safe distance.'

Elder-Main nodded obediently and stepped into the revolving door. As it whispered and spun he disappeared into the house. But, simultaneously, someone else breezed from the house into the arboretum and stepped out of the revolving doors.

'Celandine!' said Carnacki.

Celandine Gibson stood there, eyes closed, swaying slightly as she walked towards them, then past them, with the ethereal demeanour of the sleep walker. The Doctor watched her with interest. 'It would appear that Elder-Main was right after all,' he said.

Carnacki shot a furious glance at the Doctor. 'She may be in a somnambulist trance, but there's no reason to suppose she's the killer.' Zoe wasn't so sure. The eerie demeanour of the young woman put her in mind of Lady Macbeth. Celandine had now reached the fountain, her long dress rustling as she floated along. Carnacki turned and hurried after her. Zoe looked at the Doctor. He showed no inclination to follow.

'What do we do?' said Zoe.

'There are conflicting schools of thought on that. Some maintain that it is dangerous to waken a sleepwalker. I'm not sure that's true. But in any event I think our best bet is to allow the person most familiar with Celandine to attempt the awakening.'

Carnacki and Celandine were now out of sight in the green depths of the arboretum. For a moment there was no sound, then Carnacki began to shout, 'Doctor, come quick!' Zoe and the Doctor raced towards the sound of his voice and found themselves ducking back into the green shadows of the poppy bower. Here they found Carnacki standing, distraught and helpless as Celandine kneeled among the poppies, her body bent over Jamie's. It took Zoe a moment to realise what she was doing.

Celandine was kissing him.

'Doctor! Stop her! It's the kiss of death, remember?' Zoe looked at the Doctor, who showed a maddening reluctance to take action. So she plunged forward herself, only to be brought up short as he seized her arm. 'No, look,' whispered the Doctor.

As Celandine held her mouth pressed to Jamie's, a warm red glow appeared on his skin, spreading out from his mouth to cover his entire face and vanish under his hairline. Zoe saw the same ruddy glow appear on his hands and fingers, which began to slowly wriggle. Jamie was stirring in the young woman's embrace.

'He's waking up,' said Zoe.

Celandine released Jamie, allowing him to sag back under the carpet of poppies. But he only disappeared for a moment before slowly rising up on his elbows, his eyes flickering blearily open.

Celandine's eyes remained shut as she withdrew deeper into the bower where she stood, silent and still. Carnacki moved to join her, touching her face and hands. She made no response. There was no sign that she was aware of his presence, or the presence of any of them.

Zoe kneeled beside Jamie as he groaned and blinked. She brushed red petals out of his hair. 'He seems to be all right!' She looked at the Doctor. 'Why did her kiss wake him up when it . . .'

'Put the others to sleep?' suggested the Doctor. 'Permanently.'

'Killed them. Yes.'

'There's no proof of that,' said Carnacki fiercely, turning away from Celandine. 'We only have the testimony of that butler.'

'No, it is true,' said a voice. It was an unearthly voice, low and supple and sibilant, like the wind stirring through leaves. Zoe felt the hairs crawl on the back of her neck. She turned and stared in the same direction as the others. At Celandine.

Celandine Gibson, or what had once been Celandine Gibson, stood in the verdant shadows of the bower. Her face was growing visibly paler as she spoke. 'It is true. I brought death to the Upcotts,' she said. Her voice was the soft, moist rustling of a breeze among green leaves. 'I sent each one into an endless sleep with the touch of my lips.' Zoe stared at her. Celandine seemed to be growing taller and slimmer before her eyes. Zoe wondered if she was hallucinating. 'Do the rest of you see this?' she said.

Carnacki stared, rigid with fear. Celandine was definitely growing thinner. Her limbs stretched with a slow vegetal subtleness, becoming thinner and paler and more attenuated. Her fingers extended and grew emphatically white, like pale shoots stretching through loam. Her face, too, thinned and stretched. Her lovely eyes swam closer together as the bones of her skull altered, narrowing and rising at the temples like a bulb swelling with growth. All over her body, her skin became moistly smooth and brilliantly pale, taking on the gleaming opalescent white of a freshly peeled onion. Beads of milky liquid dewed her face and hands, gleaming. From this pale sweat came a heady musky odour, like a garden releasing all its scents at the end of a hot summer's day.

Carnacki made a choking sound. 'She's transforming . . .' he said.

Celandine's neck and shoulders rose from her dress, growing more supple and narrow as she grew taller and increasingly pale. The curve of her white breasts came into view, two perfect gleaming pearly vegetable globes. Then Celandine's dress slipped off altogether, sloughing away like the discarded husk of a seed pod. Her perfect pale body rose like a ripe shoot from the descending pile of discarded clothing. As she grew slimmer and taller her undergarments slipped off, too. Her nipples were revealed as perfect pink rose buds sprouting from the inhumanly smooth domes of her milky breasts.

All over her body the tiny drops of exudate appeared, milky and thicker and more sticky than sweat. Like sap, thought Zoe, her head swimming.

Celandine's hair was changing. Growing drier and straighter, its colour turning from blonde to the palest of white. Soon its texture was like dry fine corn silk. Her lovely eyes, once a penetrating deep blue had now deepened to black, with no distinction between iris and pupil.

On her pale torso her navel vanished, growing shallow, then smoothing out and disappearing into the smooth white expanse of skin, as though smoothed away by the hand of an invisible sculptor.

Carnacki's voice was shaking. 'She's half plant, half woman,' he whispered. Zoe felt pity for him as the man stated the obvious. She knew that Carnacki's attempt at analytical detachment was his only means of hanging on to his sanity, as he saw this happen to the woman he loved.

The plant thing's face had taken on some of the blankness and simple figured geometry of the petalled faces of the poppies. Her lips were a symmetrical slash of red. Her eyes gleaming black dots centred in moist white. Her white hair drifted and stirred, the finest of gossamer responding to the slightest air current. The flower smell was intoxicating, almost overpowering.

'I brought death,' said the plant thing. 'But I can bring life as well. My kiss brought your friend back to life.' She nodded at Jamie, who was trying, unsuccessfully, to rise from his bed among the poppies. Every time he managed to get to his knees, he sank down again.

The Doctor stepped forward, fearlessly approaching the thing that had been Celandine Gibson. 'Careful Doctor,' said Carnacki, his voice trembling. 'What is she?'

The Doctor stood in front of the plant creature, smiling and bowing politely. 'Celandine is a medium. She is now possessed by the life force of a plant.' He turned back to the thing, confronting her unafraid, and addressed her as an equal. 'Isn't that correct?'

'I am the spirit of the poppy,' replied the petal face, speaking in its unearthly voice. 'I am responsible for the killings here. I have brought eternal sleep to the appointed ones.'

'You murdering fiend!' said Carnacki. He seemed to have finally accepted the distinction between the woman he loved and this thing that inhabited her body.

'Don't waste your wrath,' said the Doctor. 'She is neither good nor evil.' The Doctor turned to the plant woman. 'You're an impersonal force whose power has been misused by human beings.'

'Just like the blood of my pods,' it whispered.

'Opium you mean. Yes, exactly like opium. A substance which is neither good nor evil, but can be either depending on the will of the humans who use it.'

'Now my mission here is over,' said the plant woman. She closed her glistening black eyes. On the other side of the bower, Jamie lurched to his feet then sat abruptly back down again in a shower of petals. 'What happened to me?' he muttered. 'I was with this fella and he was being ever so pleasant and then all at once,' Jamie's voice grew hot with indignation, 'He stuck me with a needle!'

'Doctor look!' cried Carnacki. They turned to see that Celandine was growing unsteady, her knees sagging. Her eyes flickered shut. As she began to topple over, her appearance started to change. 'She's reverting, thank God,' said Carnacki. He plunged down beside her, up to his knees in poppies, and embraced her cool pale nudity. The faint greenish tinge that underlay the milky white of Celandine's skin began to disappear. Then the subtle hint of human colour began to assert itself in the white skin, like paint flowing through milk, deepening it and staining it. Freckles appeared on what had been inhumanly flawless skin.

Simultaneously Celandine's hair began to darken, returning from the unearthly corn silk to the thickness and lustre of golden blonde human hair.

The natural colour of her skin returned and her navel appeared again on her smooth torso as if the finger of an invisible sculptor was gently indenting pink clay. Carnacki began to snatch frantically at her discarded clothes, throwing them over her naked body. Zoe was touched by his obvious solicitude for Celandine, although he did seem more concerned about getting her dressed again than anything else.

Celandine had by now reverted to a normal human form and her eyes opened. She looked up at Carnacki and began to sob. He embraced her and comforted her, trying to conceal the tears that gleamed on his own face. 'What happened to me?' sobbed Celandine.

'You're all right now, have no fears,' said Carnacki, stroking her hair. Jamie came up and stood beside them on unsteady legs. 'What's going on Doctor? Why did that girl kiss me?'

'Oh go back to sleep Jamie,' said Zoe. She was amazed at how quickly she'd got over her profound relief at finding Jamie safe and reverted to finding him annoying. 'We'll explain it all later.' She turned to the Doctor. 'What did she mean by saying her mission here was over?'

'She was the instrument of the Chinese astrologer's revenge. Her task was to mete out retribution to the foreign devils who despoiled the Celestial Kingdom. Her mission was to kill the Upcotts. The entire bloodline. So when she says her mission is over, I can only take it to mean that the last of the Upcotts is gone. Pemberton must be dead.'

'On the contrary, Doctor.'

They all turned to see Pemberton Upcott standing in the opening of the bower clutching a rifle with a long blue steel octagonal barrel. 'As you can see, I have managed to escape from the cursory arrangement of custody imposed on me and arm myself from my family's considerable arsenal.'

'He's the one, Doctor!' said Jamie. 'He's the Sassenach that stuck me with the needle.'

Pemberton Upcott nodded. 'I knew this would happen. They're clever fiends those Chinese. It's all in my great grandfather Roderick's diary.'

'The Emperor's Chief Astrologer and his magic.'

'That's right, Doctor. All about how he put a curse on Great Grandpa and his family. Our family. A curse set to be activated after a hundred years.'

He nodded towards Jamie. 'So when this Scottish individual arrived, a walking anachronism from another century, I knew it had begun. He was the first manifestation of the curse. But I didn't know if killing him would set things right.' He frowned, showing his uneven yellow teeth. 'Or only make them worse.'

'So you put that muck in my veins,' snarled Jamie.

Pemberton nodded. 'Yes, to keep my options open by keeping you in a state suspended somewhere been life and death. A narcotic limbo. And, that achieved, it seemed safe enough to leave you here, embowered, while I waited for the next manifestation of the curse. The Chief Astrologer predicted that our family would enjoy a hundred years of wealth and good fortune, only then to face a terrible reckoning. We would lose everything. On the principle that it is worse to have something and then lose it than to have nothing. It makes the suffering all the keener. Cruel fiend, your Chinaman.'

Chapter Twelve

Pemberton Upcott led the Doctor and the others out at gunpoint, taking them from the steamy warmth of the arboretum into the wintry garden, to the very edge of it, where the ground ceased and the star strewn void began. 'This is far enough,' he said jovially. 'Can't go any further, really, can we?' He kept the rifle pointing at them steadily as he glanced over his shoulder into the infinite abyss that began a few feet away. 'At least, I won't be going any further.'

'What does he mean?' said Celandine. Carnacki held her tight and didn't reply. Jamie and Zoe stared at the Doctor. 'I think he intends to send us over the edge,' said the Doctor in an instructional tone of voice.

'Quite right, Doctor. The perfect means of disposing of you and the others. All the witnesses in one go. Vanished without a trace. No *corpus delecti*, no crime, no recriminations.' Pemberton braced his rifle against the crook of his arm so he could aim it one handed, then reached down with his free hand and clawed up a large clump of earth. He turned and threw it into the void. The clod of earth described a lazy trajectory, sailing outwards and downwards, disappearing into the void, falling forever, or at least until it was out of sight. He smiled with approval and turned back to his captives just as the Doctor was drawing a silver whistle from his pocket.

'Put that away, Doctor, or I'll blow your head off.'

'Very well,' said the Doctor affably, 'if you insist.' He slipped the whistle back into his pocket. Pemberton nodded with approval. 'Now who will be the first to step off the edge?' He smiled at them over his rifle. 'Come now. No volunteers? What about you, Doctor? Come, I thought you'd be eager for the experience. Surely you should embrace it in the spirit of scientific enquiry.'

'I will,' said the Doctor quite calmly, peering over the edge with interest.

'No!' cried Zoe. Jamie growled something incoherent and menacing. The Doctor silenced them with a look, then turned to Pemberton. 'But before I go, answer one question. Why did you desecrate the grave of your ancestor Roderick?'

'I didn't. The lightning strike was genuine. Perhaps another manifestation of the curse. What happened to his remains I don't know.' He raised his gun. 'Now kindly step off the edge of the world, Doctor.'

'Sorry,' said the Doctor. 'Did I say one question? I meant two. My other question is simply this. Why do you think you were spared?' Pemberton frowned impatiently over the sights of his rifle. 'Spared? What do you mean?'

'The curse was intended to wipe out all surviving descendants of the opium trader Roderick Upcott. And they are indeed all dead. With the conspicuous exception of yourself.'

'I have no idea, Doctor. Now kindly step off the edge or I'll blow you to hell where you're standing.'

'The Doctor's right,' said Carnacki. 'The curse hasn't run its course yet. You're a condemned man, Upcott.' Pemberton turned his rifle to Carnacki. 'I'll take my chances,' he said. 'And since you chose to speak up, you can be the first to go, Mr Carnacki.' Celandine Gibson gave a small cry of despair and hugged Carnacki fiercely. 'No,' she cried. 'If you won't let go of him,' said Pemberton, 'the two of you can go together.'

'I suspect you may be the one who is going somewhere,' said the Doctor. 'And if you look towards the house you'll see the figure who will be accompanying you.'

'A feeble trick, Doctor,' said Pemberton.

'Not at all. Why do you think the house and its grounds were transported into this void, this colossal cosmic emptiness where it now hangs?'

'The workings of the curse, I suppose. I don't know. Anyway, you're just playing for time. Now be a good fellow and step off the edge.'

'Before I do I should point out that the curse did indeed bring us into the void. But it did so for a specific reason, so that certain natural laws would be in abeyance.'

'Of course,' murmured Carnacki.

'This is all very dull, Doctor,' said Pemberton.

'And certain extraordinary things could happen. So that certain entities could appear among us. Look behind you, Pemberton.'

But Pemberton stubbornly kept both the rifle and his gaze aiming unwaveringly at the Doctor. It was Zoe who looked towards the house and realised the Doctor wasn't bluffing. She gave a small cry and everyone else turned to look, including Pemberton.

An apparition was stalking towards them, across the snow, out of the shadows of the house. Even at this distance it could be discerned that, despite being human in general form and outline, there was something terribly wrong with it. Zoe took a step closer to Jamie. 'What is it?' he murmured, a note of fear in his voice. 'It's some kind of trick,' rasped Pemberton Upcott. Carnacki grinned fiercely and said, 'I knew it!'

'What is it?' repeated Jamie.

The Doctor regarded the approaching thing with calmness and equanimity. 'The embalmed cadaver of Roderick Upcott, I'd say.'

'Tosh!' spat Pemberton. 'It's some kind of trick.'

'Not at all,' said Carnacki, laughing. 'It is your ancestor, animated by an unholy spark of life. I knew it.'

'You're lying,' said Pemberton. 'You're . . . ' But he fell silent as the shambling figure drew close to them, its appearance unmistakable. Zoe didn't want to look, but she found she couldn't look away. It was Roderick Upcott, no mistake. Or what was left of him after the efforts of the undertakers, and the better part of a century underground. The animated cadaver was walking, or rather limping, towards them with a loose shambling gate that allowed it to slither forward through the snow. Zoe had at first thought there was something deformed about it, a hunchbacked appearance to its silhouette, but now as it drew closer she saw that clinging to Roderick's back was the equally embalmed and equally living cadaver of his pet monkey. Just legible on the pale skin of Roderick's chest was his livid dragon tattoo.

The Doctor watched this ghoulish apparition with scholarly fascination, then turned to Pemberton and remarked cheerfully, 'I suspected the curse had yet to complete itself. It seems that instead of the spirit of the poppy, your own ancestor is to be your executioner. The old destroying the new. It has a certain ironic justice, wouldn't you say? Just the sort of thing that might have appealed to the Imperial Astrologer when he planned to punish the foreign devils.'

Pemberton wasn't listening to the Doctor. He was staring at the approaching figure of Roderick, his eyes wide with terror. He gave an inarticulate, wordless cry as the shambling thing closed in on him. He aimed his rifle and fired, but of course that didn't do anything to the man who was already dead. It merely caused the monkey on his back to twitch and gesticulate in fury.

Pemberton operated the bolt on his rifle and fired again, with equal futility. He shifted the bolt once more, then seemed to realise that it was useless. He held the rifle up like a club, ready to defend himself from the inexorably approaching thing. He took a step back, then another step, then he backed right over the edge of the precipice. The cadaver of Roderick Upcott stopped and watched as Pemberton roared, windmilling his arms, sending the rifle flying, before finally losing his balance and falling backwards into the swirling cosmic fire of the void.

The others raced to the edge and looked down, but there was nothing they could do. Pemberton was a tiny doll, falling silently, first moving, then still. Then finally out of sight. Zoe looked up and saw the corpse of Roderick Upcott regarding them with its empty eye sockets. The mummified form of the Capuchin monkey clung to his shoulders and put its wizened face next to his, as if consulting with him, or about to kiss his cheek. Zoe felt her stomach heave.

'Is it over?' said Jamie anxiously, looking at the Doctor, who pursed his lips thoughtfully. 'Well, Roderick has been brought back from the dead by the curse to witness the destruction of the dynasty he founded. And that would seem to be conclusive.'

'He doesn't show any signs of returning to his long sleep though, Doctor,' whispered Carnacki. Celandine gave a low moan. 'Look,' she said. 'The tattoo!' Zoe had already seen it. The tattoo on Roderick's chest had begun to deepen in colour, returning to the vivid shades she remembered from their encounter in Canton. As the rich colours of the tattoo re-emerged Zoe thought a similar rebirth would spread over Roderick's cadaver, returning him to the state of a living man. But far from it. The jade green of the tattoo pigments spread over the dried skin of the cadaver, and even over the gnarled figure of the monkey that clung to his back, squirming as though in torment. Within a few seconds the tattoo had expanded to cover every inch of the skin of the dead man and his pet. Then it shimmered, the green tattoo ink seeming to take on the iridescence of living scales. A rainbow corona of colours shimmered over Roderick and Sydenham, and reflected on the snow as it shifted through the spectrum from green to bright red.

'Red,' said Carnacki urgently, 'Like the marks on the dead bodies.'

'Yes,' said the Doctor. 'The red dragon.'

The bodies of Roderick and his monkey were both bright red now. As if affected by the new colour, they began to twitch and move strangely. 'Oh no,' said Jamie. 'They're getting bigger.' For a moment Zoe refused to believe him, but then she saw it, too. The man and the monkey were twitching and expanding, their bright red flesh flowing like warm red candle wax. They flowed together, coalescing, so that it was no longer possible to tell where the man ended and his pet began. The formless red shape rose up on two squat pillars of legs and stretched towards the night sky, lumpish arms extended, twin heads canted back in agony.

'What's happening Doctor?' said Jamie.

'It's transforming.'

'Into what?' demanded Jamie. But Zoe had already guessed, even before the long tail, the sharp wings, and the predatory jaws began to take shape. It was a dragon.

Just like the one on the forehead of each murder victim. But bigger. Much bigger. Zoe stared up at it as it rose against the dark sky, towering over them, its scales bright as red lacquer, its fangs like carved ivory, its mad eyes gleaming with the fire of lanterns.

Carnacki seized Celandine's hand and turned and fled back towards the house, their feet crunching on the snow. The Doctor backed away, gesturing for Jamie and Zoe to follow him. 'It seems to be ignoring us,' he said. 'But I'm not sure how much longer that will be the case.'

'But all the Upcotts are dead now,' said Zoe. 'And I don't mean to be callous, but shouldn't that let us off the hook? Shouldn't the curse be spent?'

'Not necessarily,' said the Doctor. 'The curse might have been tailored to harm everyone in the household, merely starting with the Upcotts before moving on to destroy everyone else.'

'Oh marvellous.'

'Tricky things, curses,' said the Doctor.

The dragon was stretching, as if recovering from a long confinement. Its wings rose up against the black sky and blotted out the stars. Its claws spread in lethal sprays as it pawed the snow covered ground. It moved with a rustle and a thump, its tail sweeping a wide curved shape in the snow, throwing up an iridescent frosty spray.

The Doctor and Jamie and Zoe were now a good distance away from it, and away from the edge, moving across the garden in the direction of the hedgerow maze. 'Is this where you left the TARDIS?' said Zoe, feeling a sudden warm pang of hope. 'The TARDIS!' exclaimed Jamie gleefully. 'Aye! Let's get in and get gone.'

'We can't just leave the others,' said Zoe. She was feeling a renewed confidence with the proximity of the TARDIS, and the distance they had put between themselves and the dragon. She looked back and saw it standing with its head thrown back, as if studying the stars. Then it raised its great wings and launched itself upwards. Zoe prayed that it was going straight up, to disappear into the heavens. But instead the wheeling red shape spun lazily over head and then came plummeting down, scattering snow as it landed directly in front of them. Its huge fiery eyes focused on them and it opened its wide jaws, exposing the rows of serrated fangs.

'Right, I've had enough of this,' said the Doctor. He took out the silver whistle, and blew a shrill piercing note at enormous volume. He took it from his lips and smiled with satisfaction at Zoe. 'There,' he said decisively. But nothing had happened. Zoe looked at the dragon. The sound of the whistle seemed to have puzzled it for a moment. It closed its jaws and rolled its big predatory head from side to side.

'What's the whistle for Doctor?' said Jamie.

'Nothing, evidently,' said the Doctor petulantly. He began to back away. 'Come on.'

'What do we do now, Doctor?' said Zoe.

'Try and stay out of its clutches. When I say run . . .' He didn't need to complete the sentence.

The dragon stirred its glittering red bulk. Its lantern eyes focused on them again. It took a step forward, its taloned feet shuffling through the snow. It seemed in no hurry, and it had no need to be. One step had brought it towering over them again. Zoe thought she could smell it now. It smelled like garlic and ginger and gunpowder.

'We need some kind of weapon,' said Jamie staring up at the enormous lacquered red armour of the dragon's breast. 'We might have one,' said the Doctor, smiling. Zoe turned to see that Carnacki was running up, accompanied by Celandine. They were carrying a long leather bag. It took a moment for Zoe to remember what it was. 'The lance!'

Carnacki skidded to a stop in the snow beside them. 'That's right!' he cried defiantly. 'We'll use it to slay this thing!' Celandine was fumbling with the straps of the carrying case. Carnacki bent to assist her and together they threw it open. Inside was the dull lethal length of the medieval jousting lance. 'Help them, Jamie!' snapped the Doctor.

'Now that's a proper weapon,' cried Jamie, helping Carnacki draw out the lance and aim it upwards. The dragon watched their efforts with monumental patience and what might have been detached amusement over the ambitions of these puny creatures. What could they do to harm it?

'Brace the lance against the ground,' commanded the Doctor. 'Point it upwards so that when the dragon strikes it will impale –' The rest of his words were lost as a shrill whistling scream spiralled through the air above them and suddenly the sky was alive with fireworks.

Explosions and flashes of red and green light. Golden star bursts. 'Good old Elder-Main!' shouted the Doctor. Zoe stared across the grounds towards the spirit gate. She watched the conflagration begin. First the air was filled with spinning golden flame, green streamers and red and blue cascades, climbing into the night and reflecting their colours off the snow. Then a more definitive explosion echoed towards them, bouncing off the stone face of the house, as the casks of black powder detonated. Smoke and glowing cinders rose up in clouds, revealing a broad patch of melted snow, and the crumbling ruins of what had been the spirit gate.

'So much for the source of your power,' said the Doctor, smiling up at the dragon. The fire seemed to have died in the apparition's eyes, and its great bulk seemed somehow to have lost substance. The glow had vanished from its red lacquered armour. It writhed strangely, not like a living thing, but like an inanimate object moved by the wind. And as it writhed, its scales lost their sheen and turned into coloured flakes of paper.

'It's not a real dragon at all,' said Celandine in a wondering voice. 'It's made of paper.' As they watched the dragon blew up in the air like a kite, lifted by a gust of wind until it floated in the dark sky where the sparks from the fireworks hovered like fireflies. The drifting hot cinders ignited the paper wings of the great red dragon and in a moment it was burning. The flames spread across its carcass, consuming it hungrily until all that was left was a shrivelled weightless cinder, a wraith. It blew up in the air and dispersed into dust that gradually settled, dirtying the snow.

The Doctor stirred the speckled snow with the toe of his shoe. 'The residue of the cremation of Roderick Upcott,' he said.

'Ugh, Doctor!' Zoe hastily brushed the ash off her hair and shoulders. 'Anyway, he's finally got that monkey off his back,' said the Doctor, smiling.

The smell of gunpowder was everywhere. Smoke drifted up into the dark sky and away to the edge of their truncated horizon, hanging there like heavy curtains of mist. Above them the smoke formed a dense barrier. The stars were blotted out. But as Zoe stared she could see an odd glow forming beyond the smoke, like the glow of distant banked fires. The smoke took on a faint pink hue and suddenly, with the smell of gunpowder raw in her nostrils, Zoe felt a vertiginous sense of déjà vu. For an instant she thought she would hear the slapping of the rope on a flag pole and feel the crunch of gravel under foot ... and when the smoke cleared she would find herself back in the garden of the British trade concession in Canton, where this had all begun. She looked at the Doctor. 'What now?' she said. The Doctor just smiled and shook his head.

The glow increased and the smoke drew back, like mist lifting. Suddenly Zoe knew where the light was coming from. She felt tears of relief gathering in her eyes as the pale winter sun appeared from the smoke above them. She turned to the edge of the garden, where Pemberton had stepped into oblivion. But instead of a star filled void there were the rolling hills of

Kent. The garden was linked once more to the rest of the world.

A cheering crowd emerged from the manor house, blinking in the daylight. Elder-Main came hurrying across the snow to join the Doctor. His collar was black and his hair was singed, but he was grinning. 'Went off a treat, didn't it sir?'

'Well done,' said the Doctor, turning to Carnacki to include him in the compliment.

Carnacki hefted the lance and said, 'A shame about that, Doctor. I fancied a bit of St George and the dragon.' The crowd surged towards him, cheering and laughing. 'I think now would be a good time to withdraw,' murmured the Doctor. They moved away as the crowd closed around Carnacki and Celandine. The last Zoe saw of Carnacki, he was being slapped jovially on the back and shaking hands with both hands.

She hurried after Jamie and the Doctor as they moved towards the maze on the far side of the house, trudging through the snow, their breath fogging on the cold clear air. 'Is it really over?' said Jamie.

'Well, it seems that the curse has been lifted,' said Zoe. 'A century old Chinese spell is spent.'

The Doctor wiped ash from his lapels. 'Yes. The foreign devils have finally been vanquished.'

The End

Already Available

DOCTOR WHO: TIME AND RELATIVE by KIM NEWMAN

The harsh British winter of 1962/3 brings a big freeze and with it comes a new, far greater menace: terrifying icy creatures are stalking the streets, bringing death and destruction. An adventure featuring the first Doctor and Susan. Featuring a foreword by Justin Richards. Deluxe edition frontispiece by Bryan Talbot.
SOLD OUT Standard h/b ISBN: 1-903889-02-2
£25 (+ £1.50 UK p&p) Deluxe h/b ISBN: 1-903889-03-0

DOCTOR WHO: CITADEL OF DREAMS by DAVE STONE

In the city-state of Hokesh, time plays tricks; the present is unreliable, the future impossible to intimate. An adventure featuring the seventh Doctor and Ace. Featuring a foreword by Andrew Cartmel. Deluxe edition frontispiece by Lee Sullivan.
£10 (+ £1.50 UK p&p) Standard h/b ISBN: 1-903889-04-9
£25 (+ £1.50 UK p&p) Deluxe h/b ISBN: 1-903889-05-7

DOCTOR WHO: NIGHTDREAMERS by TOM ARDEN

Perihelion Night on the wooded moon Verd. A time of strange sightings, ghosts, and celebration. But what of the mysterious and terrifying Nightdreamers? And of the Nightdreamer King? An adventure featuring the third Doctor and Jo. Featuring a foreword by Katy Manning. Deluxe edition frontispiece by Martin McKenna.
£10 (+ £1.50 UK p&p) Standard h/b ISBN: 1-903889-06-5
£25 (+ £1.50 UK p&p) Deluxe h/b ISBN: 1-903889-07-3

DOCTOR WHO: GHOST SHIP by KEITH TOPPING

The TARDIS lands in the most haunted place on Earth, the luxury ocean liner the Queen Mary on its way from Southampton to New York in the year 1963. But why do ghosts from the past, the present and, perhaps even the future, seek out the Doctor? An adventure featuring the fourth Doctor. Featuring a foreword by Hugh Lamb. Deluxe edition frontispiece by Dariusz Jasiczak.
£5.99 (+ £1.50 UK p&p) p/b ISBN: 1-903889-32-4
SOLD OUT Standard h/b ISBN: 1-903889-08-1
£25 (+ £1.50 UK p&p) Deluxe h/b ISBN: 1-903889-09-X

DOCTOR WHO: FOREIGN DEVILS by ANDREW CARTMEL

The Doctor, Jamie and Zoe find themselves joining forces with a psychic investigator named Carnacki to solve a series of strange murders in an English country house. An adventure featuring the second Doctor, Jamie and Zoe. Featuring a foreword by Mike Ashley. Deluxe edition frontispiece by Mike Collins.

£5.99 (+ £1.50 UK p&p) p/b ISBN: 1-903889-33-2
SOLD OUT Standard h/b ISBN: 1-903889-10-3
£25 (+ £1.50 UK p&p) Deluxe h/b ISBN: 1-903889-11-1

DOCTOR WHO: RIP TIDE by LOUISE COOPER

Strange things are afoot in a sleepy Cornish village. Strangers are hanging about the harbour and a mysterious object is retrieved from the sea bed. Then the locals start getting sick. The Doctor is perhaps the only person who can help, but can he discover the truth in time? An adventure featuring the eighth Doctor. Featuring a foreword by Stephen Gallagher. Deluxe edition frontispiece by Frad Gambino.
£10 (+ £1.50 UK p&p) Standard h/b ISBN: 1-903889-12-X
£25 (+ £1.50 UK p&p) Deluxe h/b ISBN: 1-903889-13-8

DOCTOR WHO: WONDERLAND by MARK CHADBOURN

San Francisco 1967. A place of love and peace as the hippy movement is in full swing. Summer, however, has lost her boyfriend, and fears him dead, destroyed by a new type of drug nicknamed Blue Moonbeams. Her only friends are three English tourists: Ben and Polly, and the mysterious Doctor. But will any of them help Summer, and what is the strange threat posed by the Blue Moonbeams? An adventure featuring the second Doctor, Ben and Polly. Featuring a foreword by Graham Joyce. Deluxe edition frontispiece by Dominic Harman.
£10 (+ £1.50 UK p&p) Standard h/b ISBN: 1-903889-14-6
£25 (+ £1.50 UK p&p) Deluxe h/b ISBN: 1-903889-15-4

DOCTOR WHO: SHELL SHOCK by SIMON A. FORWARD

The Doctor is stranded on an alien beach with only intelligent crabs and a madman for company. How can he possibly rescue Peri, who was lost at sea the same time as he and the TARDIS? An adventure featuring the sixth Doctor and Peri. Featuring a foreword by Guy N. Smith. Deluxe edition frontispiece by Bob Covington.
£10 (+ £1.50 UK p&p) Standard h/b ISBN: 1-903889-16-2
£25 (+ £1.50 UK p&p) Deluxe h/b ISBN: 1-903889-17-0

DOCTOR WHO: THE CABINET OF LIGHT by DANIEL O'MAHONY

Where is the Doctor? Everyone is hunting him. Honoré Lechasseur, a time sensitive 'fixer', is hired by mystery woman Emily Blandish to find him. But what is his connection with London in 1949? Lechasseur is about to discover that following in the Doctor's footsteps can be a difficult task. An adventure featuring the Doctor. Featuring a foreword by Chaz Brenchley. Deluxe edition frontispiece by John Higgins.
£10 (+ £1.50 UK p&p) Standard h/b ISBN: 1-903889-18-9

£25 (+ £1.50 UK p&p) Deluxe h/b ISBN: 1-903889-19-7

DOCTOR WHO: FALLEN GODS by KATE ORMAN & JONATHAN BLUM

In ancient Akrotiri, a young girl is learning the mysteries of magic from a tutor, who, quite literally, fell from the skies. With his encouragement she can surf the timestreams and see something of the future. But then the demons come. An adventure featuring the eighth Doctor. Featuring a foreword by Storm Constantine. Deluxe edition frontispiece by Daryl Joyce.
£10 (+ £1.50 UK p&p) Standard h/b ISBN: 1-903889-20-1
£25 (+ £1.50 UK p&p) Deluxe h/b ISBN: 1-903889-21-9

DOCTOR WHO: FRAYED by TARA SAMMS

On a blasted world, the Doctor and Susan find themselves in the middle of a war they cannot understand. With Susan missing and the Doctor captured, who will save the people from the enemies from both outside and within? An adventure featuring the first Doctor and Susan. Featuring a foreword by Stephen Laws. Deluxe edition frontispiece by Chris Moore.
£10 (+ £1.50 UK p&p) Standard h/b ISBN: 1-903889-22-7
£25 (+ £1.50 UK p&p) Deluxe h/b ISBN: 1-903889-23-5

Coming Soon

DOCTOR WHO: EYE OF THE TYGER by PAUL McAULEY

On a spaceship trapped in the orbit of a black hole, the Doctor finds himself fighting to save a civilisation from extinction. An adventure featuring the eighth Doctor. Featuring a foreword by Neil Gaiman. Deluxe edition frontispiece by Jim Burns.
£10 (+ £1.50 UK p&p) Standard h/b ISBN: 1-903889-24-3
£25 (+ £1.50 UK p&p) Deluxe h/b ISBN: 1-903889-25-1
Published November 2003

DOCTOR WHO: COMPANION PIECE by MIKE TUCKER & ROBERT PERRY

The Doctor and his companion Cat face insurmountable odds when the Doctor is accused of the crime of time travelling and taken to Rome to face the Papal Inquisition. An adventure featuring the seventh Doctor and Cat. Featuring a foreword by TBA. Deluxe edition frontispiece by Allan Bednar.
£10 (+ £1.50 UK p&p) Standard h/b ISBN: 1-903889-26-X
£25 (+ £1.50 UK p&p) Deluxe h/b ISBN: 1-903889-27-8
Published December 2003

Other Telos Titles Available

TIME HUNTER

A new range of high-quality original paperback novellas featuring the adventures in time of Honoré Lechasseur. Part mystery, part detective story, part dark fantasy, part science fiction . . . these books are guaranteed to enthrall fans of good fiction everywhere, and are in the spirit of our acclaimed range of Doctor Who Novellas.

THE WINNING SIDE by LANCE PARKIN

'Who controls the past controls the future. Who controls the present controls the past.' 1984, George Orwell
Emily is dead! Killed by an unknown assailant. Honoré and Emily find themselves caught up in a plot reaching from the future to their past, and with their very existence, not to mention the future of the entire world, at stake, can they unravel the mystery before it is too late? An adventure in time and space.
£8 (+ £1.50 UK p&p) Standard p/b ISBN: 1-903889-35-9
£25 (+ £1.50 UK p&p) Deluxe h/b ISBN: 1-903889-36-7

Horror/Fantasy

THE MANITOU by GRAHAM MASTERTON

A 25th Anniversary author's preferred edition of this classic horror novel. An ancient Red Indian medicine man is reincarnated in modern day New York intent on reclaiming his land from the white men.
£9.99 (+ £2.50 p&p) Standard p/b ISBN: 1-903889-70-7
£30.00 (+ £2.50 p&p) Deluxe h/b ISBN: 1-903889-71-5

CAPE WRATH by PAUL FINCH

Death and horror on a deserted Scottish island as an ancient Viking warrior chief returns to life.
£8.00 (+ £1.50 p&p) Standard p/b ISBN: 1-903889-60-X

KING OF ALL THE DEAD by STEVE LOCKLEY & PAUL LEWIS

The king of all the dead will have what is his.
£8.00 (+ £1.50 p&p) Standard p/b ISBN: 1-903889-61-8

GUARDIAN ANGEL by STEPHANIE BEDWELL-GRIME

Devilish fun as Guardian Angel Porsche Winter loses a soul to the devil . . .
£9.99 (+ £2.50 p&p) Standard p/b ISBN: 1-903889-62-6

TV/Film Guides

BEYOND THE GATE: THE UNAUTHORISED AND UNOFFICIAL GUIDE TO STARGATE SG-1 by KEITH TOPPING

Complete episode guide to the middle of Season 6 of the popular TV show.
£9.99 (+ £2.50 p&p) Standard p/b ISBN: 1-903889-50-2

A DAY IN THE LIFE: THE UNAUTHORISED AND UNOFFICIAL GUIDE TO 24 by KEITH TOPPING

Complete episode guide to the first season of the popular TV show.
£9.99 (+ £2.50 p&p) Standard p/b ISBN: 1-903889-53-7

THE TELEVISION COMPANION: THE UNAUTHORISED AND UNOFFICIAL GUIDE TO DOCTOR WHO by DAVID J. HOWE & STEPHEN JAMES WALKER

Complete episode guide to the popular TV show.
£14.99 (+ £4.00 p&p) Standard p/b ISBN: 1-903889-51-0
£30.00 (+ £4.00 p&p) Deluxe h/b ISBN: 1-903889-52-9
Published August 2003

LIBERATION: THE UNAUTHORISED AND UNOFFICIAL GUIDE TO BLAKE'S 7 by ALAN STEVENS & FIONA MOORE

Complete episode guide to the popular TV show.
£9.99 (+ £2.50 p&p) Standard p/b ISBN: 1-903889-54-5
£30.00 (+ £2.50 p&p) Deluxe h/b ISBN: 1-903889-55-3
Published September 2003

Hank Janson

Classic pulp crime thrillers from the 1950s.

TORMENT by HANK JANSON

£9.99 (+ £2.50 p&p) Standard p/b ISBN: 1-903889-80-4

WOMEN HATE TILL DEATH by HANK JANSON

£9.99 (+ £2.50 p&p) Standard p/b ISBN: 1-903889-81-2

To order copies of any Telos books:

Telos Publishing, c/o Beech House, Chapel Lane, Moulton, Cheshire CW9 8PQ, England • Email: orders@telos.co.uk • Web: www.telos.co.uk